HERBIE GOES TO MONTE CARLO

by Vic Crume

From the Walt Disney Productions' film written by Arthur Alsberg and Don Nelson and based on characters created by Gordon Buford

SCHOLASTIC BOOK SERVICES
NEW YORK • TORONTO • LONDON • AUCKLAND • SYDNEY • TOKYO

Copyright © 1977 by Walt Disney Productions. This edition is published by Scholastic Book Services, a division of Scholastic Magazines, Inc., by arrangement with Walt Disney Productions.

12 11 10 9 8 7 6 5 4 3 2   7 8 9/7 0 1 2/8
Printed in the U. S. A.

GOES TO MONTE CARLO

Chapter 1

What a sight!

Swinging safely in a cargo net from the big ship's unloading crane, Herbie had a bird's-eye view of the busy docks below. In fact, he could see quite a lot of the port city of Le Havre, France.

Herbie is a white Volkswagen bug with a big, bright "53" painted on his hood and sides, and the view wasn't quite what he'd expected. A small frown crept between his pistons. Not a race track in sight! Odd! Herbie was sure that Jim Douglas, his driver, and Wheely Applegate, his mechanic, had brought him across the Atlantic Ocean especially to race. Then the cargo net started to descend, and Herbie spotted his friends down on the docks. He'd soon find out where he'd be taking them!

While the net was thumping Herbie to an easy four-wheel landing, a French customs official was thumping the official stamp on Jim's and Wheely's passports. The official also glanced at a picture of Herbie and added a third thump.

"Destination — Monte Carlo," he said in a business-like voice and shoved the passports across the counter. The two Americans hurried off, anxious to claim the third member of their racing team.

"There he is!" Wheely sang out when he saw the VW. "Look out Europe! Here comes Herbie!" They broke into a fast trot.

They knew their little white bug, Herbie, was someone extra special. Wheely knew every inch of Herbie — from front to back bumper — and he had never located anything unusual tucked away in the fierce little racer, but he and Jim were sure that Herbie had a mind and a heart of his own hidden *somewhere*. No wonder they rushed to the unloading dock to meet Car 53.

Herbie's engine hummed joyously. It was clear to him that Jim and Wheely didn't know the way to where they wanted to go — wherever it was. But Herbie was glad to be moving again.

Jim, at the wheel, had no time to admire the French towns and countryside between Le Havre and Paris. He was too busy following Wheely's road instructions. And Wheely, trying hard to pronounce French words and names, barely glanced up from the map spread across his knees.

Therefore it came as no surprise to Herbie when the threesome slowed to a stop in a barnyard filled with wildly squawking chickens, quacking ducks, and, worst of all, angry geese that came hissing straight for Herbie's tires.

"Hey! Where're you going?" Wheely looked up startled.

Jim sighed. "Somehow I think we took a wrong turn back there."

"Yeah." Wheely frowned. "The road sure is missing. Well, how do you say 'gangway' in French?"

"Same as you do in English," Jim replied calmly. He looked at the milling throng of barnyard citizens and blasted a few solid honks.

Not a goose honked back, and Herbie, always glad to be on the move, zoomed into a U-turn in search of the missing highway. Once he'd found it, he whizzed the miles away. If the road led all the way to China he would gladly make the trip, taking only necessary stops for gas.

But Jim and Wheely had other plans. And after a good many curves, turns, stops, and starts, Herbie came to a standstill right in the middle of a colossal traffic jam — in front of Paris's famous *Arc de Triomphe*.

"That's the Arch of Triumph," Wheely grumbled. "But this is a disaster."

Herbie loved it though. Nothing pleased him more than that wonderful perfume called "gasoline." Paris was going to be exciting!

The next day, Herbie sensed no improvement in Jim and Wheely's attempts to get where they wanted to go. Once again, Wheely had a map spread across his knees.

He frowned. "First we find the Rue Boissere a Rue de Lubeck a droit a Place d'In."

Jim groaned. "Wheely, will ya give it to me in English?"

"Sure," Wheely replied. "We're lost."

Jim suddenly felt the steering wheel pull hard to the left. "Hey, Herbie! What're you doing?"

Herbie made a sharp turn. "Herbie! Where're you going?" Wheely called.

"He's getting us un-lost," Jim laughed. "See that gendarme? He's heading for him."

"John who?"

"Jon-darm. That's French for 'policeman.'"

Herbie whirled up to a stop. "Excuse me, officer. We're looking for the Trans France Race Exposition. Could you help us?" Jim asked.

The gendarme smiled. "Ah, oui, oui!" He waved toward the end of the block, then pointed

4

to a turn to the left. "That is to be some race!" he exclaimed.

"And you're looking at the winner right now," Wheely grinned, patting Herbie's dashboard.

The gendarme's eyes widened. *"This!* This car the winner?" He thwacked his hand against his stomach and laughed loudly.

Immediately Herbie reacted to the gendarme's rude behavior. He rolled back a bit to position his left rear wheel next to the gendarme's highly polished shoes. *Spritz!* Oil spurted out and Herbie spiritedly moved on, leaving a dismayed gendarme gazing down at the extra polish on his leather-clad foot!

The gendarme's instructions to turn left sent the threesome into a very narrow street. Up ahead, a big armored truck was parked tight to the curb. Two guards carrying guns and a heavy metal box jumped out of the back of the truck to escort a small, very neatly dressed gentleman to a doorway.

Because of the size of the truck and the clusters of curious onlookers, Herbie barely had space to edge slowly forward. If Jim, Wheely, and Herbie understood French, they would have understood the crowd's curiosity.

"What's in the box, the museum payroll?" someone in the crowd called out.

Monsieur Ribeaux, curator of the museum, answered indignantly. "No! No! It contains the most magnificent diamond in the world! *L'Etoile de Joie!*"

"How about just one little peek?" another member of the crowd cried out jokingly.

Monsieur Ribeaux shook his head. "Precisely at one o'clock, you and all of Paris will be able to take 'the peek.' Now, stand back!" He strode proudly up to the museum entrance.

Not even Herbie, who was a good guesser, could know how important the famous Star of Joy diamond was to be in his life.

A short distance ahead, the street ended at an open square. A big banner fluttered across the sky — TRANS FRANCE RACE. At last! Herbie's carburetor fluttered excitedly. "Lead me to the track, fellas!"

A mini-type auto show seemed to be going on instead of a race. Racing cars, drivers, mechanics, and race fans crowded the square. For a moment, Herbie's spirits drooped. No track in sight! But his interest picked up as a man's voice came over a loudspeaker: ". . . and here, fresh from his triumphs on the European racing circuit, is Bruno Von Stickle. He'll be driving his powerful Lazer 917 GT coupe."

There was loud applause from the crowd as a

tall, blond man bowed and smiled in a rather haughty way.

"Ah ha!" the voice continued. "I understand the American entry, Jim Douglas, is just arriving." The man looked down at his notes. "He will be racing in — in — uh, a most unusual entry." Then the man, who seemed to be the master of ceremonies, signaled to one of his helpers. "Would you send him up this way, please?"

Herbie angled into the throng of sleek, stream-lined racing cars looking a little like a plump, oversized marshmallow wearing a number "53" as a decoration. The crowd turned, looked, and right away a solid laugh roared out.

Wheely looked puzzled. "Something funny must have happened."

Jim nodded. "I think it's us."

"*Us*?"

"Us," Jim repeated, and stopped Herbie in a spot between Bruno Von Stickle's much admired entry and a formidable Pantera II with its driver, Claude Gilbert, standing alongside.

"How about giving Jim Douglas and his part-ner, Wheely Applegate, a nice warm welcome?" the MC called.

The crowd politely clapped hands, but it was no deafening roar. The MC looked over at Car 53. "This little car has been the toast of America." He glanced back at his notes. "Let's see, when was your last win?"

"Twelve years ago," Jim answered promptly. This time the crowd roared with laughter.

Wheely quickly took the microphone. "Only because that was our last race!" he exploded.

Jim leaned forward. "And we're making a kind of 'comeback.' That's why being in this race is so important to all of us." Then he quickly added, "Of course, we won't be 'coming back' very far if we don't qualify first."

Wheely stared at Jim in amazement. Forgetting he still had the mike, he blurted out, "*Qualify*? Are you kidding?" He flushed and turned back to the crowd. "Uh — don't let my partner's modesty fool you. There isn't a finer tuned, cleaner engine anywhere."

Bruno Von Stickle laughed. "Must be pretty easy to keep it clean. What do you do? Drop it into the washing machine with your socks?"

Wheely tried to be good-natured about the crowd's reaction to this put-down. "Appreciate your humor, Von Stickle," he said. Herbie knew that Wheely really wanted to say, "Von Pickle."

"Don't you folks worry about this little washing machine . . . I mean, car. It's a real jewel!" he exclaimed proudly.

Chapter 2

Another real jewel was not far away. In the museum near the square, L'Etoile de Joie rested on a small velvet pillow atop a pedestal. The pedestal stood in the exact center of a square formed by four tall posts that were meant to keep viewers at a distance from the valuable diamond. It glinted so brilliantly in the light that the beauty of paintings and statues along the walls of the room was dimmed.

Duval, a museum guard who had been assigned to watch over the diamond, looked worriedly at Monsieur Ribeaux, the museum curator. "But is this not too much responsibility for one man? I am nervous just thinking of the crowds who will be coming to see it."

Monsieur Ribeaux smiled. "One man? Let me put your fears to rest. You and the finest security system ever devised will keep it safe. I shall show you."

He took a small computer from his pocket and extended the antenna attached to it. "All in the computer. Listen." As he punched a series of numbers, musical sounds like those of a pushbutton telephone could be heard. "This device alone would keep the diamond safe from the grasp of a thief."

The guard looked puzzled. "But, Monsieur, one would have only to reach over like this — " He touched the diamond. Instantly an alarm rang out, and at the same moment the guard was hurled to safety by Monsieur Ribeaux. And in the nick of time, too! For a large metal cage came crashing down from a trap door in the ceiling.

"You see?" Ribeaux pushed more numbers on the computer, and the cage rose back up to the ceiling. Duval stared up in amazement. He struggled to his feet. "But *how*?"

"The pillow is sensitive to the heat of the hand. When it gets close to the diamond the cage is released."

Duval shook his head. "I still worry. What if the cage struck an innocent person. Or what if the thief had cold hands?"

"Nonsense! Cold hands!" Monsieur Ribeaux frowned.

"Sorry, sir," the guard replied humbly.

"Very well. I'm glad you understand. Now — I

shall place this bell jar over the pillow." He stepped forward, put the glass cover in place, then stepped back. "Watch, now." He punched out another group of numbers.

"What does that do, sir?"

"I am engaging a system of electric-eye beams that surround the pedestal."

"Beams?" Duval reached out his hand. "I don't see any be — "

Again an alarm sounded. Again Ribeaux pulled Duval to safety as the heavy cage crashed down. "Is it possible I picked the wrong guard?" he asked in an icy voice.

"No, no. Please, Monsieur. I now understand. It will never happen again."

At the push of the computer buttons, the cage rose. "There is one thing yet I must show you," said Monsieur Ribeaux. "We shall join the other guards and go just outside the entrance of this room."

When the men were lined up to his satisfaction, Ribeaux tapped out more numbers on the computer. "And now," he said importantly, "that entire room is a trap. The mere falling of a cigar ash on the floor would activate the alarm." He took care to fling his arm across Duval just in case the guard took a notion to test the security system a third time. But Duval had learned his lesson. The door was quickly closed and the men stepped into the hallway. Monsieur Ribeaux motioned toward the door. "To be opened every ten minutes as a security check."

"I promise you, sir. I shall guard it as I would my daughter's honor. But pardon, sir. You have forgotten to give me the computer and the numbers."

"I did not forget! They were put in my trust and they will remain with me. This is the only copy in existence!"

Poor Duval paled. "How am I to do this guarding, then?" he asked timidly.

Monsieur Ribeaux looked scornfully at him. "I shall be here myself. Naturally."

Duval sighed in relief. "Oh. You are not leaving the building. Of course, sir. I am stupid for the moment!"

But as the men left, he scratched his head worriedly. "I am still stupid. I do not understand all this push-push, crash-crash." He glanced at his watch. In ten minutes he must make his first safety check. Nervously, he began to pace the long hallway.

Almost as Duval was walking away from the door, two of the statues inside the small electronically guarded room opened. From each, a man stepped out.

The smaller of the two squinted his narrow-set eyes at his pocket watch. "Right on schedule, Quincey. Now just ten steps to a million dollars — our share!"

"Yeah? Or one step to Devil's Island," his burly partner replied. "Don't forget what happens, Max, if anything touches that floor." Quincey reached under his coat and lifted out a nylon lasso. Expertly he swung the loop around a heavy bronze statue across the room. He tied the other end to the pillar behind him and pulled the rope tight. It passed safely across the bell jar without breaking the radar beams.

Max took out a small notebook. "Not too fast, Quincey. Electronics has the answer right here. This little notebook is our passport to a big future — not to Devil's Island."

But Quincey didn't wait. "Thanks, I'd sooner put my trust in this bit of rope." Quickly he grabbed the lasso with his hands and ankles, and inched himself along toward the bell jar.

Max watched for only a second before taking out a small computer like the one Monsieur Ribeaux had used. He drew up the antenna, checked the notebook, and rapidly punched out numbers. Quincey was still inching along when Max walked calmly past him.

"Quincey, get down from there." He patted the notebook. "It's all in here. Silly not to use it. The

Man worked it all out for us, didn't he?"

Quincey plainly had his doubts about computer magic. He slowly lowered one foot to the floor. No alarm clanged out. He walked up to Max, who stood by one of the four guard posts. "So far, so good," he said grudgingly. "But I'm going to use the spray I brought along to check for any radar beams."

Max shrugged. "You needn't bother, but spray away."

Instantly, the spray made light beams show. "See!" Quincey exclaimed. "We could have blown the whole act right here!"

"Sure, I see," Max grinned, punching the next set of numbers. "First you see it — now you don't." The beams disappeared and he confidently stepped over to the bell jar.

L'Etoile de Joie flashed and glinted on the velvet pillow. Carefully, Max lifted the glass cover and set it on the floor.

"Some hunk of rock!" Quincey's voice dropped to an awed whisper.

"Yeah," Max nodded. "You could live a lifetime without setting your eyes on a rock like that — let alone getting your hands on it."

At the word "hands" Quincey reached for the diamond. Like lightning Max snatched his partner's hand. "Patience! The pillow's the trap.

Now, one last set of numbers and it's ours. Wait a minute."

He studied the notebook and frowned. "Now why can't the Man write a zero that looks like a zero?"

Quincey bent to look at the notebook. "I'd say it's a six, not a zero."

"Or maybe it's a nine," Max scowled. *"We can't take a chance."*

"Your Double-X and his electronics!" Quincey exclaimed in disgust. "Well, I don't trust anybody. *I* came prepared." He took an accordion-like mechanical claw from his pocket. "Old ways are still the best ways."

Max checked his pocket watch. "You got six minutes till the guard checks the door. Get on with it!"

Skillfully, carefully, Quincey guided the claw until the prongs closed around the diamond. The beautiful gem lifted from the pillow. Both men took a deep breath. Success! *No!* A tiny bell sounded. Quincey's grip on the claw jerked. Down went L'Etoile de Joie — straight to the velvet pillow.

Flushing red, Max took out his pocket watch and pressed the alarm to "off." Quincey glared. "Aren't you ever going to get that thing fixed?" Nervously he began once more to guide the claw toward the diamond — and one million dollars!

"Patience. Patience," Max said softly.

"Tell that to the guard,"Quincey snapped. "We got two minutes left."

"Let me have that claw," Max said calmly. "I'll do it."

Max, great believer in patience and calm, was not as patient or calm as needed. For the second time the diamond fell back. "Almost had it," he muttered angrily. "One more try."

"There's no time!" Quincey cried. "That guard is practically at the door now."

"You want the diamond, don't you?"

"Yeah! And there's one way to get it!" His hand shot out and swept the diamond from the pillow. Instantly the alarm sounded, and almost as quickly, the metal cage dropped.

But this time, one of Quincey's "old ways are best ways" saved them. The heavy cage balanced and came to rest on the nylon lasso!

In a rush of fear, the pair galloped for the windows at the back of the room. Without hesitation, they crashed through the glass — L'Etoile de Joie going with them!

Monsieur Ribeaux and Duval were in time to see only two pairs of vanishing heels.

Ribeaux rushed to the empty velvet pillow, Duval right at his heels. *"Diable! C'est terrible!"*

16

he roared, and stamped his feet in rage. Above them, the nylon rope snapped. Crash! Down came the cage, trapping a stunned Duval and an enraged Monsieur Ribeaux neatly inside!

Over at the mini-Expo, the crowd was not aware of the big excitement going on at the museum. And Wheely, patting Herbie's hood, was not even aware that the crowd that had been listening to his stories about Herbie had quietly moved on to more exciting cars.

"I tell you — this little guy has won some of the biggies on the American circuit." He lovingly stroked Herbie's number 53. "Daytona, Virginia Beach — talk about burning rubber!" He looked around. "Well! Talk about talking to yourself!" He only hoped Herbie hadn't noticed! What an insult!

He looked over to see Jim walking a collision course toward a very pretty girl, not watching where she was headed either. Sure enough! Jim smashed straight into her. The crash helmet she was carrying dropped to the pavement.

Swiftly, he bent to pick it up. So did she. *Clunk*. Their heads met solidly.

"Oh, sorry!" Jim exclaimed. He grinned. "Just trying to prove chivalry isn't dead."

The girl rubbed her head. "Thanks. But one

more bump like that and one of *us* will be."

"Well, I'm certainly sorry." Jim handed back the helmet. "Maybe you ought to be the one wearing this instead of your boyfriend."

"Boyfriend?" the girl said coldly. "This helmet happens to be mine."

Jim stared. "Wait! Don't tell me. You're Diane Darcy! I've seen you on the sports page. Dover Speedway last month, wasn't it? You ran a whale of a race."

Diane replied only briefly. "Thanks."

"Finished third. That was really great."

"What's great about finishing third?" she asked icily. "Oh, I guess you meant — great for a woman."

"I didn't say that. You did."

"No, you didn't. But that's what you were thinking, wasn't it? *Just* a woman."

Jim grinned. "*Just* a woman? Not guilty."

Wheely walked over. "Hey, Jim."

Turning quickly, Jim knocked Diane's helmet to the pavement for the second time. Wheely picked it up and handed it to Diane. She nodded and marched off.

Jim looked admiringly after her as she walked away. A sudden anxious look came over Wheely's face. "Come on, Jim," he said. "Don't get involved — if you know what I mean. Herbie's waiting for us."

18

Jim didn't move.

"Listen — Herbie's waiting for us, and — well, I'll make a deal with you right now. Paris may be the City of Love but it can be the land of heartbreak too. Don't forget that! I'm willing to forget the girls if you will. Herbie is the one who needs us. Nobody — but *nobody*, had a good thing to say about him. The little guy must be lonesome. Come on."

"Forget the girls?" Jim sighed. "That's some sacrifice."

"I'm willing to make the sacrifice until after the race. How about you?"

"Okay, Wheely," Jim laughed. "It's a deal. Let's get back to Herbie. I'll just wait in Monte Carlo for Diane to catch up."

"Diane? Was that Diane Darcy?"

"Right."

Wheely frowned. "If I remember it right, she drives a great car — a Lancia." He shrugged. "Oh, well, Herbie can take on a Lancia or any other car any day of the week. We sure will be waiting for Miss Diane Darcy! Right in Monte Carlo!"

Jim couldn't keep his mind on what Wheely was saying to one stray Frenchman who had paused to view Number 53.

"Well, we're coming into the big right-hand turn, see?" Wheely waved his arm about.

"Dropped him into third gear and jumped on it. Took three cars just hittin' the straight — then back into fourth and we were flying . . . takin' seven or eight grand. Well, we blew off the lead car about a hundred yards from the finish and won goin' away. How about that!"

The Frenchman shrugged and spoke politely. *"Je ne comprends pas Anglais."*

Wheely turned to Jim. "What'd he say? I didn't understand."

"That's okay," Jim sighed. "Come to think of it, I'm not sure I did."

Bruno Von Stickle, who had been standing nearby, stepped over. "I understood. You Americans are great storytellers. What's even better — you believe your own stories." He laughed and strolled on.

Wheely glared after him. "If that turkey's looking for trouble, he's going to get it. Bigger they come, harder they fall!" He thumped his fists together.

"As long as he doesn't fall on us. We'd better make sure this comeback *is* a comeback."

Over the P.A. system, a voice boomed out. "May I have your attention, please. Those drivers who are in the first qualifying rounds at the track this afternoon should be leaving in ten minutes. Repeat — Those drivers . . .

Bruno Von Stickle came strolling back. "Will you be qualifying at the track, Douglas? Or," he added, nodding toward Wheely, "just in his imagination?"

Wheely turned angry red, but before he could think of a biting reply, Herbie took over. Swiftly he took aim and fired a giant water window spray straight across the proud Von Stickle face.

Not knowing where the stream of water came from, Von Stickle whirled around, wiping at his eyes. Wheely leaned forward, skinny fists clenched. "Attaboy, Herbie. You just saved that guy from a terrible beating."

Von Stickle was still mopping his face when from somewhere near the square came the sudden wailing of French police cars. "It's from down the street," somebody said.

"The museum!" another cried out. "Something's wrong. Look at those police cars swarming up."

"Hey!" Wheely yelled. "Something sure is up. Barricades. They're starting to put up barricades right there at the end of the street."

Chapter 3

Not only police cars, but dozens of Paris citizens came popping out into the street to see what had happened. This was the best thing that could have happened for Max and Quincey. Unnoticed, they were able to edge their way quickly into the square and join the mini-Expo crowd.

"Attention, everyone," the MC called out. "Police bulletin! Police bulletin!"

With everyone else, Jim and Wheely turned to see a police chief step up with a bullhorn. "Attention!" he boomed out sternly. "Nobody is to leave the area. I repeat — *nobody*."

Wheely jerked off his helmet. "What's he mean — nobody is to leave? How'll we qualify if we don't get outta here?"

"Going to be tough," Jim agreed. "We'd better have a word with the chief." He strode off and Wheely followed, leaving Herbie to wait it out alone.

A crowd clustered around the MC and the chief. "What's the trouble?" Jim called out.

The MC answered. "The famous diamond, L'Etoile de Joie, has been stolen from the museum."

Over the bullhorn the chief made it official. "There has been a theft in the museum, ladies and gentlemen. Everyone will be searched before leaving the area."

Jim raised his arm. "Might as well start with us."

More gendarmes were arriving to assist their chief. Max and Quincey exchanged worried looks. Quincey clenched the precious diamond. "No use both of us being caught. Here — you take it."

Max's narrow face tensed as he felt their million-dollar treasure being pressed into his hand almost as the gendarmes were closing in.

He edged back — right into Herbie's gas-tank cap. His eyes glittered. "No need for either of us to be caught."

Deftly, he popped the tank top. In a split second, L'Etoile de Joie was out of sight. There was nothing Herbie could have done about it if he'd wanted to. Besides, he had his mind on qualifying, and the approaching gendarmes meant nothing to him.

But as Max and Quincey exchanged triumphant

looks, a horrible thing happened. Herbie's engine kicked over. *Whizz!*

From velvet pillowed, electronic security to the privacy of Herbie's gas tank, away went L'Etoile de Joie in the unsuspecting care of Jim, Wheely, and Herbie.

"We may never see it again!" Quincey moaned.

The passing MC caught Quincey's words. "Oh yes you will," he said comfortingly. "It will be in a showroom at the Champs Elysees at four this afternoon."

"Thank you," Max said politely. "We'll be there. It is a car to keep an eye on. Yes?"

The MC grinned. "Number 53? Well, everybody has a favorite, I guess." He went on his way.

In the office of Police Inspector Bouchet, Monsieur Ribeaux paced back and forth in near-hysterical tears. He wrung his hands and gulped, "I ask myself!"

"Be calm, Monsieur, please," Inspector Bouchet said soothingly.

"Calm! I ask myself! What more could I have done? And I ask *you*. Why? Why? Why? Every precaution was taken. 'Be calm,' you say. How is 'calm' possible when that beautiful diamond entrusted to me is gone? Gone!"

Inspector Bouchet glanced at his assistant, Detective Fontenoy, a bright-faced young officer who idolized his chief. He looked back to the frantic Monsieur Ribeaux and sighed. "Please, Monsieur Ribeaux! You simply must stop crying. It will ruin your health."

"Ruin my health!" sobbed Ribeaus. "If I stop crying I'll kill myself."

Detective Fontenoy leaned forward to hand him a handkerchief. "I assure you, that won't be necessary, Monsieur."

"Thank you, thank you." The miserable Ribeaux dabbed rapidly at his streaming eyes.

Detective Fontenoy was not sure if the robbery victim was saying thank you for the handkerchief, or for the assurance that he need not end his life. But he had no doubt that Monsieur Ribeaux was feeling terrible. "Inspector Bouchet will have that diamond back for you like that." Cheerfully, he snapped his fingers.

Inspector Bouchet looked toward his assistant. "Thank you for your confidence, Fontenoy, but I'm afraid I'll require just a bit more time."

Ribeaux burst into a fresh flood of tears. "More time? But every moment that passes could be taking the diamond farther away."

The young detective could not stand seeing such grief. "No, no! Every moment that passes will be bringing the Inspector closer to the solution. Think of his great reputation!"

Ribeaux's tears shut off as though Fontenoy had turned a tap. But the detective reached for his dampened handkerchief too soon. The museum curator burst into another fit of tears. There was little hope for the handkerchief now as Ribeaux was using it not only for dabbing purposes, but also for chewing.

"The Inspector's reputation!" he sobbed. "Do you know where *my* reputation is? I'll tell you where it is. Twenty-five years — out the window with that diamond!"

The Inspector stood up. "Please control yourself," he said almost sternly. "This robbery was carefully planned, but we will do all in our power to put the diamond safely back in your hands."

At these words, Monsieur Ribeaux seemed to grow even more desperate. "Oh, if I could only believe you." Sobbing loudly, he tugged with all his strength on the borrowed handkerchief. *Rip!* Hem to hem, it tore neatly down the center. Through a blur of tears he stared at what had only a moment before been a handkerchief. Pitifully, he held out the two strips.

There were signs that more grief was on the way. Detective Fontenoy spoke hastily. "That's all right. You keep it. I have another."

*　　*　　*

Bright posters and signs advertised the qualifying rounds of the famous Trans France Race. But the scene on the outskirts of Paris was made really exciting by the high-powered cars — Ferraris, Lamborghinis, Porsches, as well as MGs and Triumphs.

Drivers were already prepared for the start of the next qualifying heat when Jim, Wheely, and Herbie came circling up. Jim drove over to a race official who was checking off cars against the list on the clipboard he carried.

"Douglas and Applegate," said Jim.

"Yes, Mr. Douglas. You and Mr. Applegate are in the heat following this one. Good luck!"

"That's the same heat I'm in, Douglas," Bruno Von Stickle called over from the pit, where his crew was putting last-minute touches on the Lazer. "You're going to need more than luck. You're going to need wings." He laughed. "I'm sending you and your four-wheeled relic back to your rocking chairs."

He turned away, picked up a hose, and began to put water in the Lazer's radiator.

Wheely, his Adam's apple working up and down, his face pink, shouted over at Bruno's back. "Well, you may be in for a little surprise, Von Stickle."

Bruno half-turned. He grinned. "I've seen your

little surprises. And they are little."

That was too much for Herbie. He'd been hearing nothing but insults to himself and his best friends all day! As Bruno squeezed the release on the hose nozzle and the water began to pour out, Herbie rolled quietly back — just far enough back to rest a wheel across the hose.

The water stopped flowing. Puzzled, Bruno lifted out the nozzle and looked into it. Herbie rolled forward. Out shot a geyser of water, soaking Bruno from head to toe.

Wheely's angry flush changed to hilarious red. There was Bruno, once again spluttering water. Jim, along with Wheely, tried to keep from exploding with mirth. He called over, "You can count on an even bigger surprise when the race starts, Bruno!"

It was time for the drivers to pull their cars into starting position, and Jim began to move Herbie through the pit area. A sleek, shining Lancia was coming in their direction. Herbie jolted to a stop, pulled his wheels hard to the right, and swung back to follow the Lancia.

"Hey, Herbie!" Jim yelled.

The Lancia was positioned in the starting line. It seemed to glow all over. The more it glowed the more Herbie trembled.

Wheely called out excitedly, "Hey, Herbie! What are you nervous about? This isn't even our qualifying run."

Every car in the starting line roared off as the starter's flag went down. And Herbie went *up* — right up on his rear wheels, throwing Jim and Wheely back against the seats.

"Herbie," Jim yelled again. "Where you going?"

It was all too plain where Herbie was going . . . right after the Lancia. The driver had pulled into a comfortable lead and Herbie had to weave left to right to pass every single racer to reach his goal.

"Darn it, Herbie! You could get us disqualified!" Jim tried to shift down. He tried to jam on the brake. Nothing worked! As Herbie barely squeezed between two cars to catch up with the Darcy entry, Wheely closed his eyes in panic.

"He could get us killed!" he gasped as the Lancia zipped on ahead to take the far turn and Herbie raced up alongside. He leaned dangerously close.

The driver tried to wave off Number 53. Jim and Wheely did their best to show they didn't have Herbie under control.

He certainly wasn't! His windshield wipers flipped madly back and forth, and his antenna shot up and down. Then he gave off a long, low wavering sound. Only Herbie knew it was his best wolf whistle.

"What was *that?*" Wheely gasped.

"I think you got him tuned too fine," Jim answered shakily, holding hard to the wheel.

Herbie did another wolf whistle. Unseen by either the drivers or Wheely, the Lancia blinked her headlight lids in a flirty way.

That was all Herbie needed! He was inspired. It was time for music, and music was something Herbie had. To everybody's horror, a waltz came blaring out on Number 53's radio. Even more alarming was Herbie's swaying in time with the 3-4 beat. He zipped and zagged across the track before the Lancia driver's amazed and angry gaze.

"Herbie!" Jim shouted. "Are you flipping your lid?"

Wheely's thin face tensed. "Don't mention that. You'll be giving him a new idea."

But the Lancia had the new idea. The little beauty zigged and zagged directly behind Herbie. She forgot the whole idea of the race — to get ahead of Number 53. Angrily, her driver shook a fist as car after car zoomed past the waltzing pair.

"Herbie's out of his mind!" Jim groaned.

"He's out of his mind, all right." Wheely's face was grim. "Over that luscious Lancia."

Jim took a quick, anxious look at his partner. "Wheely's gone crazy," he thought, alarmed. "He's just been too involved with Herbie."

But in the next second he wondered if all of them hadn't gone crazy. Herbie went into a 180-degree spin, and wound up bumper to bumper facing the Lancia, waltzing in reverse.

"Impossible! Impossible!" Wheely shrieked. "I'm telling you — Paris and women have got him. I'm gonna have to warn him the same way I did you — like father like car!"

"Don't blame me! You're the mechanic. How come he can put himself in reverse gear? How come — *everything*? Wheely, you got to tighten him up somewhere."

At that moment the Lancia was pulled to a stop at the side of the track. Herbie broke off in mid-waltz, swung up beside it, and stopped. Wheely, dizzy from his musical ride, hopped out and lurched first in one direction, then another. Jim managed to turn off the radio, and Wheely came to an unsteady stop.

The driver of the Lancia bounded out of the car and strode angrily toward Herbie and Jim.

"See what you've gotten us into, Herbie? That guy's ready for a fight — and I can't blame him." Jim jumped out, hoping he could keep his voice calm. "Easy now! I'm terribly sorry, buddy," he said earnestly. "Something just went — "

Diane Darcy ripped off her helmet. "What do you mean, *buddy*!!?"

Stunned, Jim stared at her stormy face. "Diane!"

"You . . . you . . . you . . . "

"Jim Douglas," Jim said quickly. "And I'm terribly sorry."

"Sorry! Come *on*. You think that because I'm a woman driver you can get away with anything you please? Well, I'm not a pigeon for your fun and games! I've had it with you clowns."

"No! Honest — I'm not the clown. It was Herbie, I swear."

Diane glanced toward Wheely, who was still staggering around trying to get his balance. "You're blaming your dizzy mechanic?" she asked coldly.

"Oh, no. Herbie's the car." Jim swallowed. "You see, he's more like a person. Now I know that sounds funny, but — "

"*Funny*? Crazy is more like it! We'll settle this with the race officials."

Settle it she did.

"What were you doing out there, Douglas?" the race official asked sternly.

"Well, it's pretty hard to explain, sir — "

"Not for me, it isn't," Diane's voice bit in. "He

doesn't want women in competition. He doesn't want a woman in the race."

The race official tried not to groan. "Look, Miss Darcy — you'll be given another chance to qualify. We're terribly sorry."

"You're sorry. He's sorry. Everybody's sorry. But I didn't qualify, did I?" She spun on her heel and stalked off.

The race official looked down at his clipboard. "If you expect to qualify, Douglas, you're up now."

Back again in Number 53, Wheely gave Herbie's dashboard a small spank. "You heard that, Herbie? Forget that powder puff and get your mind on racing."

Among the cars lined up for the start were Bruno Von Stickle's Lazer GT and Claude Gilbert's Pantera II. Herbie was wedged between these two powerful cars. Bruno smiled across in disdain. "Hey, Gilbert. Look who comes in the middle of us — the cheese in the sandwich."

The two drivers winked at each other.

"Sandwich, huh!" Wheely seethed. "Well, this is where the cheese chews up the pumpernickel!"

The starter's flag dropped. Bruno and Gilbert got the jump on Herbie, sandwiching him in, not letting him through. And when Bruno's Lazer GT moved over, it accidentally nicked Herbie's front end. Herbie slid off the track and into the dirt. Before the dust settled, he'd come to a standstill, headed in the wrong direction. Other racers roared past.

"Where'd they go?" Wheely asked frantically, peering through the dust.

Jim pointed backward. "That way. Your pumpernickel and that French rye just made mincemeat out of us. Man! I really got suckered. I'm rustier than I thought."

He turned the wheel and got started in the right direction. Herbie began to pick up speed. One by one, he passed other cars until he was in third place. Gilbert's Pantera II was in second, and the Lazer GT was in the lead. Gilbert cagily weaved back and forth to keep Herbie from passing. Then Jim dropped down in the turn, shot by the unsuspecting Gilbert, and took off after Bruno Von Stickle. Herbie might have made it a win right there for Jim and Wheely. But back at the starting line a race official was clearing up the schedule for Diane Darcy's second try. "Tomorrow at two, then, Miss Darcy."

"At two," Diane repeated. "This time, just make certain there's no little circus car doing a waltz in front of me." She shifted the Lancia into gear and started down the road that ran alongside the fenced-off track.

Jim, never more determined to win, and Wheely, grinning at the very thought of how Von Stickle's ever-smiling face would change when they passed him, got the shock of their lives. Herbie's steering wheel turned so sharply it was wrenched from Jim's hold. And as Herbie veered, Wheely was almost tossed into Jim's lap.

"Hey, Herbie!" Jim yelled. "What're you doing?"

Wheely righted himself. "It's her again. He's after his great love!"

At top speed, Herbie headed along toward the road Diane Darcy was driving. Alas! He was thwarted in his mad dash to romance. A closed gate separated the side road from the track, and behind it, watching fans blocked his view. He skidded to a stop. The Lancia was gone. Gone!

But Herbie's spirits weren't as sunk as Jim's and Wheely's. Wheely's chin was trembling. "Well, at least we lost to a Lancia."

"Not to mention to a Lazer GT," Jim said gloomily. "And the first qualifying round."

Unhappily, the partners shook their heads. "Well, back to Paris," Jim sighed. "Herbie's due at the showroom at four."

Chapter 4

Quincey, right on time at the showroom where the cars that came to qualify for the big Trans France Race were on display, was getting nervous.

Car Number 53 still wasn't there. Max had left to make a phone call about this to Double-X.

By the time Max showed up, Quincey was feeling worse than nervous. "You get hold of Double-X?" he asked.

Max nodded. "He wasn't happy."

"Who is!" Quincey exploded. "Where's that dumb little car?"

"Patience, Quincey." Max stepped over to the MC. "Excuse me, sir. Some very impressive racing cars here. But — er — I don't seem to see the little VW."

"Oh, the Douglas car. It'll be here. Patience." The MC smiled and walked away, leaving Max feeling cross to hear his own advice being used on *him*.

Quincey glowered. "If I hear one more person say 'patience' . . ."

"Well, you'd better have it now," Max snapped back. "If we don't show up with that diamond, Double-X is gonna mark the spot where we get buried."

Quincey grinned. "Don't start digging our graves yet. Take a look behind you."

Max turned. Entering the showroom from the garage area came Jim, Wheely, and Herbie. The partners got out of Number 53 and strolled off to look over the competition.

"Come on, Max! Let's grab it. And don't tell me 'patience.' "

"Sure," Max growled. "Grab it in front of a hundred witnesses? We need a plan."

Over a microphone came the voice of the MC. "Attention, everyone. We'd like to show you a film of the route the racing cars will be taking to Monte Carlo. Will someone please put out the lights after I pull the drapes?"

Max nudged Quincey. "I think someone has just given us our plan."

But before the MC pulled the drapes closed, a sleek Lancia slowly passed by the showroom windows. Herbie's quick headlight blink went unnoticed in the daylight glare of the room. Then, drapes closed, lights darkened, the color film rolled.

The MC's voice filled the room. "Some of the finest machines you have seen here will be among those testing the grueling route stretching through the streets of Paris, twisting through the French Alps, and finishing in Monte Carlo. Naturally, the streets along the route in Paris will be roped off from traffic—otherwise, the racers might never make it out of this city."

The crowd laughed politely, and Quincey whispered to Max, "Now what are we waiting for?"

"Plenty of time . . . plenty of time," Max whispered back.

Not in Herbie's opinion. Quietly, the little car backed toward the garage doors he had entered just a few minutes before. He disappeared into the darkness of the corridor as the MC continued to hold the crowd's attention. "From its exciting start at the foot of the Eiffel Tower . . . the route will take them across the river . . . and racing down the Champs Elysees."

"That's a race I'd like to see," Quincey whispered.

Max muttered back. "You can watch the re-run from Tahiti. Come on — now. Just back up quietly. Edge back to the VW. I'll follow."

"The cars," the MC explained, "will be passing Place Vendome, Place du Carousel, and finally arriving at the outskirts of Paris."

By this time Max and Quincey were close to Herbie's former parking spot. No steady light from the screen reached that corner of the showroom. Quincey muttered, "We're here. I'll just back up to the gas tank. Nothing to it. You stand in front of me."

"Here! I got something!" he murmured excitedly. His hand squeezed down.

"Monsieur," a muffled voice replied. "You have my nose."

A flash of light from the screen revealed for a split second a bent-over janitor, dustpan and whiskbroom in hand.

Only the darkness spared Quincey the dirty look Max fastened on him. "Keep going!" he growled.

They backed farther away as the MC was explaining that the racing cars were now in the French countryside. "Having left Paris," he said, "you'll see these cars really pick up speed. The challenge of the French country roads can be diminished only by the challenge of the famous French Alps."

"It's just not here, Max," Quincey whispered as the crowd *oh'd* and *ah'd*.

"Of course it's here. A car doesn't disappear by itself," Max whispered back.

"These peaks," said the MC, "and narrow winding roads will test the endurance of even the sturdiest cars. For those who survive this stretch, there remains the final dash for Monte Carlo. And for someone victory is just —"

CRASH! Lights went on. There lay Max and Quincey, sprawled on the floor, a large display rack of racing trophies rolling around beside them.

"My head!" Max groaned. "It's broken!"

"Patience!" Quincey snapped.

In turning with the rest of the crowd to see the cause of the noise, Jim and Wheely saw more than that. Or less, perhaps. Herbie was gone!

"I can't believe it!" Wheely groaned. "Come on, Jim. We gotta track him down."

Parked in front of a sidewalk cafe, Diane Darcy's Lancia awaited her return. Diane was not in sight, but there were customers at several small tables by the window.

A fussy little waiter stopped at one table to take an order. He looked up from his order pad in time to see a driverless VW, marked "53," pull up to face the Lancia. Its windshield was mud-splashed, and before the waiter's unbelieving eyes, the wipers began to work furiously back and forth. Its engine revved as though to attract attention. "Impossible!" he muttered.

The customer snapped his fingers. "Waiter! Can I get some service here? Forgive me for waking you up, but I wish to order."

"Pardon, Monsieur. Of course."

At that moment, Herbie let loose with his version of a wolf whistle. Luckily for the waiter, he could not see that the Lancia's headlight lids opened a bit, then quickly closed. The poor man might have fainted dead away! As it was, he tottered off to have the order filled.

Crossing the street, two men carrying a large mirror paused between the Lancia and Number 53 to check an address. Herbie took one look at his muddied appearance and moaned. That passing truck had *really* ruined his usual dapper look. Quickly he backed away, shot out into the street, and roared around a corner. In no time, he found just what he was looking for — a large circular fountain. He drove himself in and sped around in a circle. Then, sure he was his usual sparkling self, he headed back for the cafe, pausing only to gather an attractive bouquet from a flower bed along the return route.

The waiter came back with his customer's order just as Herbie, now clasping flowers between bumper and fender, greeted his beloved. He gently flipped the bouquet into the air, and the Lancia caught it on her outside rear-view mirror. Tray in hand, the waiter stood still as a statue, eyes fixed on the driverless cars.

"Waiter — please! Are you here or are you there? Let's have my order. It has aged quite enough!"

"Pardon!" As he bent to fill his customer's glass, he saw Herbie start slowly down the street, followed by the Lancia. The sight was too much! Swiftly the waiter reached for the glass he had just set on the table and gulped the contents down to the last drop.

"Etes-vous cuckoo?" the astonished customer gasped.

"Oui!" the waiter gasped back. *"Cuckoo!"*

Diane Darcy made her way toward the front of the cafe. Her eyes rounded in horror. No Lancia.

"Waiter!" she cried out. "My car! It was parked right out there."

"A little blue and yellow car?"

"Yes. It's gone."

"Ah, yes. It is gone," he nodded, eyes staring.

Diane looked at him sharply. What was wrong with the man? "Did you see who took it?"

He scarcely blinked. "Uh — not exactly," he murmured.

Jim and Wheely came hurrying along the walk. They spotted Diane just as she spotted them. "You!" she burst out angrily. "I should have known I'd see you. You and trouble go together."

"Look, Diane — we're missing our car. You haven't seen it, have you?"

"*Your* car! Who cares about that silly bug! My *Lancia* has been stolen."

The waiter seemed to come to life. "Your — your . . . I saw them both."

Diane spun around. "Then you saw who stole them."

The waiter shook his head. "You would not believe. I do not. No one would. I think they steal each other!"

Jim and Wheely exchanged quick glances. "I believe it," Wheely muttered, and Jim grabbed Diane's arm. "Come on!" He stepped to the curb. "Taxi! Taxi!" he shouted.

The waiter was not the only Parisian who was thunderstruck that day. Herbie and the Lancia cavorted playfully up and down Paris streets. Every benchwarmer and stroller in that famous city who saw the pair nearly collapsed. One gentleman cried out, "My mind! It is going!" He spoke for nearly everybody.

But no others had such frantic feelings as Jim, Wheely, and Diane. "It's like looking for a needle in a haystack," Wheely moaned. "How'll we ever find them?"

"Got me," Jim replied unhelpfully. He leaned back in the taxi.

"Look," Diane said angrily, "my life is riding on that car."

"Lady, we've a couple of things to prove, ourselves," Jim replied. He looked at Diane thoughtfully. "Say, Diane, where would you take a boyfriend on his first trip to Paris?"

Diane gasped. She glared. "I'm in no mood for any cute ways of making a pass."

"If I had romance on my mind, would I bring Wheely along?" Jim asked earnestly.

"Right!" Wheely bobbed his head. "Why would he — " He stopped and looked at Jim. "Why not?" he asked in a hurt voice.

"It's Herbie and your Lancia," Jim said, paying no attention to Wheely's question. "Either she's showing him Paris, or it's the other way around."

Diane's eyes widened. "I don't believe it," she said slowly.

"It's true. We've known all along that there's something extra about Herbie. I mean — well, you don't know him like we do. But we've been through a lot together."

"But never anything like this," Wheely added. "This is awful. I mean — Herbie isn't awful. We love him. And you've got a wonderful car, too. But — " He waved his hands helplessly. "I mean, *this* is awful."

Little did Herbie or his friend care about public opinion. The Lancia, leading Herbie a merry chase, went ducking down from the street to the banks of the river Seine.

In the taxi, the driver began laughing loudly. Diane flushed. She leaned forward. "Driver, let me out. I've had enough of this. Do you think this is something to laugh about?"

"Forgive me," he answered, slowing his cab. "I laugh at my radio here. It says two automobiles take a ride on the *bateau mouche*. A boat on the Seine, you know. They *sightsee!* Would you believe such a thing?"

Jim snatched Diane's elbow and pulled her back. "Driver! Turn off onto that bridge," he ordered sharply.

On the bridge, the three got out of the taxi. And just in time! The *bateau mouche* was gliding out from under the bridge. There, taking in the view, were Herbie and the Lancia.

Diane paled. "What — ?"

"Maybe I could explain this over dinner tonight?" Jim noted her cold stare. He shrugged. "Maybe not."

*   *   *

In a small hotel room, Quincey paced back and forth, listening to Max's half of a telephone conversation with Double-X.

"We were just backing up to the gas tank, sir, and the next thing — the whole car was gone. Yes, sir. Gone. But I guarantee we'll get it this time. We have the hotel staked out. As soon as it's dark, we grab the diamond. . . . Oh, yes, sir. I understand." He hung up.

"Guess he's pretty mad, huh?" asked Quincey.

"Oh, no." Max replied. "He just said the next time the car disappears, we disappear."

In another hotel room, Jim looked at a French newspaper picture of Herbie. CAN CRAZY CAR COME BACK?

"I don't know if you can, Herbie," Jim sighed.

"Twelve years — that's a long time. The pressure's really on. Sure hope we can handle it." He looked up as the door opened and Wheely came in.

"All taken care of, Jim. I had a little straight talk with Herbie. Had to straighten him out. I don't mind having a car that's got a heart, but there's one thing I won't tolerate — and I told him so. That's a car falling in love with another car."

Jim shrugged. "What would you want him to

fall in love with? A Goodyear blimp?"

Wheely paced back and forth. "Be serious! I just told him, 'Herbie, we're over here for one thing and one thing only — to make the biggest comeback in racing history. You gotta forget the chick. And you can do it! Just a matter of mind over metal!' "

Jim gave Wheely a long look. It might have been longer but for a knock on the door. Wheely turned the doorknob. Inspector Bouchet and Detective Fontenoy stood there. At Wheely's invitation, they stepped in.

They had hardly introduced themselves to each other when Wheely nervously said, "Look, Inspector. If there's a problem about our car cruising on the river — "

"No, no," Detective Fontenoy spoke up. "It's about the six-million-dollar stolen diamond. We — "

The Inspector interrupted his assistant. "Mr. Douglas, we're questioning everybody who was in the area at the time. Perhaps you can help us. Some little clue, perhaps?"

On the street below, Quincey and Max located Herbie. In seconds, Quincey was after the gas-tank cap. It wouldn't budge. Not only that, but Herbie rolled backward.

"Pushing the car won't help," said Max.

"Push? Who pushed? It musta rolled."

"Then put on the brakes."

Quincey tried. "Door's locked," he said briefly.

"The window, Quincey. The window. Reach in, flip the door lock, *then* set the brakes."

Quincey pried at Herbie's wind wing and wedged his fingers in. *Snap!* Herbie clamped down hard. Quincey, yelling out in pain, jerked loose.

Max struggled with the gas-tank cap. No luck! He turned the job back to Quincey. Angrily, Quincey gave Herbie's tire a hard kick and slammed his fist on Number 53's hood.

"Step aside, Quincey. I'll hot-wire this car. That'll mean we can get it at the repair garage tomorrow." Max lifted Herbie's rear hood — to his regret! Herbie backfired briefly. Soot and carbon spewed out. Max backed away, sputtering and coughing. Herbie, with one final blast, streaked away and around the corner.

Quincey snorted. "Some hot-wiring! I suppose you're going to tell me that car just started up and drove away by itself."

Max looked grim. "No . . . and I'm not going to tell it to Double-X either. Come on."

They hurried off to the corner, still hoping to catch the VW — and one enormous diamond!

Chapter 5

Next morning, in the museum room, Inspector Bouchet and poor Monsieur Ribeaux stood near the former resting place of L'Etoile de Joie. Over by one of the hollow statues, Detective Fontenoy and a fingerprint man examined the base. Monsieur Ribeaux was near tears again.

"I did not sleep a wink last night. I was in bed. I was out of bed. I paced the floor. I walked the streets. I was back in the room. In bed. Out of bed. I tell you, I was out of my mind."

Inspector Bouchet sighed. "Yes, yes. Now, are you sure that all the security precautions had been taken?"

Monsieur Ribeaux wrung his hands. "I have searched my memory. Could I have forgotten something?"

"Inspector!" Detective Fontenoy called out

proudly. "Some trace here of a footprint. I might have overlooked it, but I heard your voice, 'Remember, Fontenoy, no clue is too small.'"

The Inspector sighed again. "Did you also hear me saying, 'Take it to the lab and have it analyzed, Fontenoy'?"

"Yes, sir. And I am doing that." He sealed some dust into an envelope and hurried from the room.

Monsieur Ribeaux flipped a tear away. "No — I know I forgot nothing. I'm as sure the security was on yesterday as I am sure it is off today." He reached out his hand to pat the empty velvet pillow. CRASH! Down came the cage, trapping the luckless Ribeaux and the Inspector.

"Fontenoy! Fontenoy!" the Inspector yelled.

Detective Fontenoy called back from the hall, "Rely on me, sir. The lab report will be ready for you by the time you reach the station!" His footsteps faded rapidly down the hall as the Inspector shook the bars in rage.

Over the public address system, the race official's voice held everyone's attention. "These are the last two qualifying rounds, gentlemen. The first three places will qualify for the Trans France."

Bruno Von Stickle chuckled. "And the others

will get to go home early, Douglas. *Bon voyage.*" He walked away.

Wheely snarled at Bruno's back, "We'll be going home as soon as we collect that trophy in Monte Carlo."

Jim looked worried. "Somehow I'm not as sure as you are."

"You wait and see," Wheely said firmly. "After that lecture I gave Herbie last night, there's going to be a new Herbie out there today."

But Herbie was not exactly burning up the track when the starter's flag came down. He was not even among the leaders coming into the first turn.

Wheely peered through the dust and exhaust smoke. "Where are we?"

"Well, since there are eight cars ahead of us, that puts us last," Jim replied.

Over at the gate, Diane Darcy came driving up. An official came up to her. "Darcy," she reported.

"Oh, yes. You're qualifying today."

"Hope so," Diane smiled.

He stepped back and waved her down the road that ran alongside the track.

Out on the track, Jim was pressing his foot right to the floor. Herbie was barely moving. "Herbie doesn't need lectures, Wheely. He needs an old-age pension. I think he's all through." Jim turned his attention to Herbie. "Now, listen, and listen good, Herbie. You and I didn't come out of mothballs to be the laughing stock of Europe. Now, if you don't get the lead out of your pants right now, I'm gonna ship you back to the States, have you stuffed, and hung on a wall in Retirement Village."

Herbie still chugged along in last place as he came up to the far turn. Suddenly his engine gunned several times. He shot forward.

"Now you're talking!" Jim exclaimed. "Is that the old Herbie, or isn't it?"

The way Herbie zoomed ahead made other cars look as though they were standing still. But on the straightaway, the lead car was still far ahead.

"One more lap, Wheely!" Jim yelled. "If he wouldn't do it for you at least he's doing it for me."

"He's not doing it for either of us." Wheely's voice was grim. "Take a quick look at what's parked up ahead by the railing. It's her. Herbie's doing it for *her!*"

Jim saw the Lancia. His jaw tightened. "I don't want to believe it. He'll come to a stop!"

But Herbie whipped right along and came abreast of the lead car. Jim's spirits soared. "I'm tellin' ya! It's the old Herbie. And he's doing it for *us!*"

Herbie rounded the final turn and crossed the finish line to take the checkered flag. Without stopping for breath, he spun a 360-degree doughnut-turn. Back he sped and came to a proud, quivering stop right in front of the Lancia. Coyly, she winked her headlight lids. Herbie winked back, then rushed back to the finish line to make everything official.

Jim shook his head. "Okay. So he did it for her — but we won."

In amazement, several official timers shook their watches. They were working, all right. Herbie U-turned back to the pits and up alongside the Lancia. Jim and Wheely got out. Race officials came running up with a crowd of excited spectators. "Congratulations! You did it!"

"Somebody did it," Wheely said numbly, a dazed look on his face.

"Who cares, Wheely?" Jim laughed. "It's 'hello, comeback' for us."

"And in record time for this track," said the race official. "You've shattered Von Stickle's record."

Gilbert, the Pantera II driver, came up. "Congratulations, Douglas. You have just won the right to taste my dust tomorrow."

"And mine," Bruno Von Stickle smiled in a down-his-nose way. "You broke my record here, Douglas — but tomorrow I turn your 'hello, comeback' to 'good-bye forever.' "

The two drivers stalked off. Wheely watched

them a second. "Bet they were drop-outs from charm school," he snorted.

Diane Darcy looked over at Herbie and the excitement surrounding him. Over the loud-speaker the announcement everybody was wait-ing for came. "Next qualifying round — five minutes."

She pulled on her driving gloves and got into the Lancia. "The idea! Driving that silly little car up to me like that!" she muttered. A fierce, de-termined look sparkled from her eyes. "I'll win. I'm going *to win!*"

Attention was now on the contenders lining up for the second race. Unnoticed, Herbie quietly drove up to the guard rail near the far turn of the track. He rested his front wheels, elbow-like, on the rail. When the Lancia whipped past him, Herbie spun his rear wheels in wild approval, then relaxed.

As Herbie's true love got the checkered flag at the finish line, officials once again looked with astonishment at their stop watches. Herbie waited at the rail until the Lancia went back to the pit stop.

"Amazing, Miss Darcy!" the race official ex-claimed.

Diane lifted off her helmet. "To me, too. I knew I had a good car under me, but — "

"You made the exact time as the Douglas car. And it's a track record!"

Jim and Wheely came up as the pit men pushed the Lancia away. "Congratulations, Diane!" Jim grinned.

"Thank you," she replied coolly. "And thank you for staying off the track. That gave me one way to prove what I can do."

Jim hesitated. "Well — it wasn't exactly *you* doing it."

Diane gave her helmet a smack. "You know — you've got a real problem about women in racing, Mr. Douglas. What is it, anyhow? We drive too slow? Or," she added sharply, "too *fast*?"

"You don't understand. That's not what I meant. It isn't you I'm talking about. It's your car. And — and my car."

Instantly, Diane turned away. "Excuse me. I don't wish to hear about you and your car again."

Jim called, "Wait, please."

"Well?"

"Herbie's not just a car. Would you believe me if I told you he has a — a — " He touched his heart. "I didn't believe it myself at first.

"Well, when a car like Herbie comes to Paris and meets a beautiful Lancia who's also got a — a — " For the second time, he could not get the word out. He stumbled on. "Well, you can't blame them for falling in — That is to say, I mean, *falling*. You know."

Diane simply stared at him. Jim sighed. "Okay. You're right. I couldn't believe it either."

Diane looked at him steadily. "When the man from the booby hatch comes by," she said, "go quietly, will you?" She walked away.

"I was just trying to warn you about your car," Jim called after her.

She looked back. "Well, let me warn you about me. I'm in the race to win. And frankly, I'd like to see you *and* your car disappear entirely." She hurried off.

Wheely spoke for the first time. "A charm school would do a great business around here."

"I tried, anyhow," Jim said sadly, "Well, we'd better start back for the city."

Herbie, fresh as a daisy despite his emotional time at the track, hummed gaily along on the outskirts of Paris.

Wheely wasn't in that good a mood. "You know, Jim — we might have a big problem on our hands."

"Yeah? What?"

"Having that Diane Darcy and her Lancia in the big race."

"She is a pretty good driver," Jim agreed.

"It's not her driving I'm worried about — it's her car. How do you think Herbie's gonna take it with his girl friend in the race?"

Before Jim could give an answer, a black sedan came whipping out from a grove of trees — right on Herbie's tail.

Jim glanced up to the rear-view mirror. "Wonder what those clowns are up to?"

The sedan, Max driving, Quincey beside him, pulled up alongside Herbie and began to nudge him off the road.

Wheely looked over nervously. "What're they trying to do?"

The answer came fast. The black car lurched into Herbie.

"Hey! WATCH it!" Jim yelled.

Max gave Herbie another swipe. Jim had to fight to keep from going off the road.

"I'll tell you what they're trying to do," Wheely shouted. "They're trying to kill us."

For the third time the sedan bumped Herbie. Quincey stuck his arm out the window and waved a gun threateningly. "Pull over," he yelled. "We want that car."

Wheely's face paled. "What're you going to do, Jim?"

"Pull over," Jim answered. Herbie slowed to a stop.

The sedan swung in behind him. Max and Quincey stepped from the black car. Herbie's steering wheel began to spin by itself.

"Herbie!" Jim gasped. "Where're you going?"

It was soon plain to all concerned. Herbie suddenly swung off the road and whizzed down an embankment. Jim held onto the wheel for dear life. Wheely, face tense, reported: "They're right behind us."

"Don't I know it," Jim gulped. "Herbie! You're going to get yourself killed. *Watch it!*"

But Herbie turned a deaf carburetor to his friend. Not only did he pick up speed, he aimed straight for a gypsy camp ahead. Wagons, trailers, tents, clotheslines, barbecue — and people.

Wheely closed his eyes. "Herbie!" he moaned.

Herbie, his rear-view mirror showing the large black car right behind him, cleverly did what the bigger car couldn't do. He aimed straight for the awnings stretched out from several tents. *Blast*! He scurried under them and out again. The big car followed — and couldn't make it. In seconds, awnings and tents draped the black sedan from bumper to bumper.

"Get it off," Max yelled. "I can't see."

That gave Herbie just the chance he needed to get ahead of his pursuer. But not far enough ahead. With canvas still clinging to his black car,

Max sped forward. There was nothing for Herbie to do but what he did — zoom right into a picnic table the gypsies had set up. Herbie roared up to the barbecue grill as though planning to go airborne any minute.

Wheely shouted. Jim held on. Herbie sailed up and over.

Behind them, the big car couldn't take wings. Weaving crazily, it struck the barbecue. And the next thing Quincey saw was the gypsies' barbecued roast, riding along in the front seat between himself and Max!

Wheely looked back, every muscle in his body tense as a steel spring. "They're still coming!"

Jim held Herbie's wheel tight — not so much in the hope of steering as to keep his balance. "I think they're trying to kill *us*!" he shouted in amazement.

Herbie swung out of the field he'd been bumping over and headed for a road under construction. A huge sewer pipe was his goal. The workmen, hearing him roar up, dropped their picks and shovels and scattered to safety. Into the pipe went Herbie! On came the big sedan. CRASH!

Herbie neatly zoomed out the far end of the pipe. Behind him, the front half of the black sedan was firmly wedged into the darkness of the pipe. Herbie didn't bother to go into one of his famous doughnut-turns to check what had happened. Pistons and gaskets, carburetor and muffler — each went about its job as though Herbie had been taking a calm drive down a country lane. Cool as a cucumber, Number 53 resumed the trip to Paris.

Chapter 6

Wheely wasn't so cool. Quivering as a result of the unexpected detour, his voice was shaking. "I didn't think she'd go that far to make us disappear."

"Who's 'she'?" Jim asked, puzzled.

"That cute little time bomb, Diane. She set us up to knock us out of the race — just like she said she would."

"Hey! Wait a minute! She didn't say that."

"Of course not," Wheely replied. "They never *say* what they mean. Oh, no. That's what makes the female of the species deadlier than the male."

"Wheely — you read that somewhere."

"Sure I did. Wish I'd said it myself. I believe it!"

"Well, I don't take that strong-arm stuff from anybody — male or female."

"Then a certain somebody better teach a certain female we know the rules of the game — before the game's over!"

Jim's face set grimly. "Don't worry. Miss Diane Darcy is going to hear about this — and soon."

Wheely and Herbie, parked in front of Diane Darcy's hotel, had nothing to do but wait for Jim. "Might as well settle back, Herbie," Wheely said. "Once Jim gets started, nothing can stop him." He looked up at the hotel windows and wondered which one was Diane's.

Nowhere near her window but at her doorway, Diane stared at Jim. Then her eyes flashed in anger. "*Me* trying to wreck your car? OUT!"

Jim didn't budge. "I didn't say you did — personally. You hired thugs to do it for you."

"Hired *thugs*!" Diane's eyes blazed. "I don't have to hire anyone to win my races for me. I'm as good as anyone on that track."

"I'm not talking about — "

"Oh, yes you are!" Diane exploded. "That's the trouble with you . . . all of you. You don't want to admit a woman can do anything as well, or better, than men. Now you listen. I've taken it from my father, my brothers, and my uncles. I've even taken it from my brainwashed mother and aunts. But I am NOT taking it from anybody any longer — and that includes you."

Downstairs, Wheely kept up his one-sided conversation with Herbie. "When ol' Jim gets started, I'd hate to get in his way. He's a regular steamroller. I know he seems like a quiet sort of guy, but when a fight's on, he never ducks it."

As a matter of fact, Jim was ducking — a vase hurled by the enraged owner of the Lancia. "Stand still, you coward!" she cried. "I'm a race driver, and I can win it on my own." She reached for a second vase.

Hastily, Jim slammed the door shut between them. Just in time! He heard the smash of breaking china and was convinced Diane Darcy didn't have to hire anyone to fight her fights. And she had had no part in hiring thugs to get Herbie off the track. There was only one track on her mind — her own.

"Then who is trying to knock Herbie out of the race?" Puzzled, he went on to meet Wheely and Herbie downstairs.

"Did you set her straight?" Wheely asked as Jim got behind the wheel.

Jim didn't answer that one. "Herbie's spending the night under lock and key. We're heading for the police station. He needs protection."

"The *police* station! Are you having her arrested, Jim? That's going pretty far!"

"No. I'm not having her arrested. But someone

is after Herbie, and we need help, don't we? You know a better place to get it?"

As they drove along, neither Jim nor Wheely noticed a crumpled black sedan parked along the curb — a black sedan they certainly had noticed earlier!

Max used a public telephone on a Paris street corner. "Double-X? I'm afraid there's been another complication." He glanced sadly at the crumpled front end of the black sedan parked nearby. "You see —"

The voice of Inspector Bouchet came crackling back. "I'm beginning to think *you're* the complication. That item should have been in my hands by now."

"Don't worry, sir. It's still in the gas tank."

"Then bring me the gas tank!" Bouchet exploded. "What are you waiting for?"

"Well, we lost them again. Don't know where they are."

"Imbecile! I give you a perfect plan, worked out to the last detail, and what do you give me? Excuses!"

"But the car has disappeared," Max said miserably.

"Impossible! Are you trying to tell me that a couple of simple-minded Americans have . . ." He stopped talking. Through the glass door of his office, he saw Jim and Wheely being directed to his door. He turned back to the phone. "Hold on. I may have a lead for you."

He quickly put his hand over the phone. Jim and Wheely knocked, then stepped into the office. "Hope we're not disturbing you, sir," Jim said, noticing the phone.

"No, gentlemen," the Inspector smiled. "Your timing could not have been better. I wanted to thank you for your continued cooperation in the matter of the stolen diamond."

"Well, it's your help we're after right now," Jim said, his voice serious.

"Somebody's out to get our car," Wheely burst out.

Inspector Bouchet looked shocked. "But that seems impossible!"

"I think they're trying to knock us out of the race. Is there some way we could put him under protective police custody for tonight?"

"That is," Wheely said anxiously, "if you're not too busy trying to find the diamond."

Inspector Bouchet could hardly hide his delight at this unexpected development. "No, no. One is as important as the other, I assure you. Uh . . . I'll be only a moment." He motioned toward the phone in his hand.

"Oh, sure," Jim replied. "Maybe we'd better wait with our car."

"Good idea." The Inspector smiled. "We wouldn't want anything to happen to it. Not now."

The second the door closed behind his callers, Bouchet picked up the phone. "Hello? The car is here. Never mind how! I will see to it that it will be at Number 32 Avenue Picard within the hour. Don't get lost on the way."

Outside the police station, Wheely patted Herbie's fender. "You're going to be in good hands, Herbie. Like Jim says, it's for your own good — and ours too."

Inspector Bouchet came out of the station and over to the curb. "Your worry is my worry, gentlemen. Rest easily. I'll take personal charge of this valuable possession."

Just as he turned Herbie's door handle, Detective Fontenoy called out to him. "Inspector!"

"What is it, Fontenoy?" the Inspector asked, as his assistant came hurrying up the sidewalk.

"Off duty or not, sir, I just couldn't sleep thinking about the diamond and how it must be weighing on your mind."

"At the moment, Fontenoy," Inspector Bouchet said coldly, "I've got a car weighing on my mind."

"And that's even heavier," Wheely said helpfully.

"For some reason," Jim explained, "somebody's been trying to knock us out of the race."

Fontenoy nodded. "With your incredible time in the trials it would not take a master of deduction like Inspector Bouchet to see that you have an excellent chance to win."

"Which is exactly why I personally will insure the safety of this automobile," his chief said firmly. "Now put your minds at ease, gentlemen. Get a good night's sleep."

Wheely fondly patted Herbie again. "That goes for you, too, Herbie."

"Right!" Jim agreed. "We've got a big day tomorrow."

Detective Fontenoy put his hand on Herbie's door handle. "No, no, Inspector! Permit me, sir! You have enough responsibility trying to find the diamond. I'll look after the car."

"Don't be ridiculous!" the Inspector snapped.

"Not at all, sir. I wish to save your — your energies." In one bound, Fontenoy was in the driver's seat and slamming the door.

"Fontenoy! What are you doing?"

"Anything for you and the force, sir." He started Number 53.

"Fontenoy . . . get out of that car," the Inspector muttered, leaning close.

But Fontenoy gunned Herbie's engine. "Leave it to me, sir. I'll keep this little car hidden so *no one* will find it."

Helplessly, the Inspector watched Herbie leap away from the curb. He looked on in horror as Number 53 sailed out of sight around the corner.

Jim and Wheely exchanged worried glances which the Inspector immediately noticed. "My best one — Fontenoy," he said in a weak voice. "Do not worry. He would guard your car with his life."

Jim and Wheely looked relieved. "Well, we both thank you a lot, Inspector," Jim said.

"Not at all."

With a good-bye wave from the steps, Inspector Bouchet went back into the police station. "My very best!" he snarled. "*Imbecile!*"

As he expected, Max called to report finding no car at Number 32 Avenue Picard.

"In the morning, before the race," answered the Inspector, "that ridiculous little car will get gasoline. When it does, you will be there to get the diamond. Now BE there." He slammed down the phone.

After checking out the starting line for the race to Monte Carlo, Herbie checks out Paris.

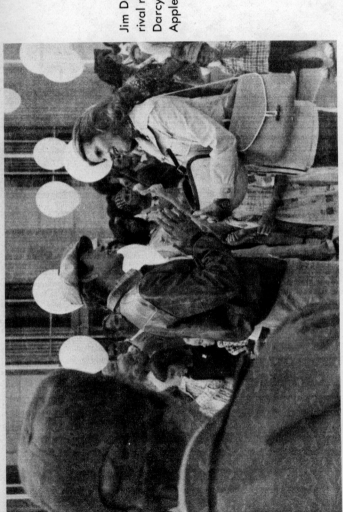

Jim Douglas meets rival race driver Diane Darcy. Wheely Applegate looks on.

Wheely and Jim push Herbie to the starting line for the qualifying race.

The racing trio can't find their cars. "I think they steal each other," an eyewitness tries to explain.

Bruno Von Stickle and Claude Gilbert taunt Jim about "little" Herbie's chances in the race.

Max and Quincey come out of hiding to steal the Star of Joy diamond. Later they hide it in Herbie's gas tank when the police close in.

Jim explains to Inspector Bouchet and his young assistant, Detective Fontenoy, that someone is following his car.

Wheely and Jim come up spouting for air after Herbie takes them slightly off course.

Lost in the Alps, Wheely decides to get out and look around.

Jim finds the diamond, and Max and Quincey find Jim and Wheely.

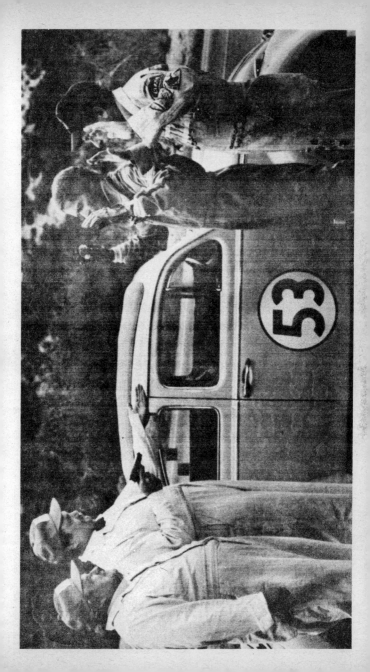

Wheely is no match for Quincey. But Herbie saves his friend and the diamond.

With the race almost won, Jim stops to rescue Diane. And Herbie saves *his* love, her Lancia.

The winners at Monte Carlo!

But the race with the diamond thieves is still not over.

Jim and Diane, rivals on the race course, get along fine together otherwise.

Chapter 7

It was a glorious morning. At the foot of the Eiffel Tower, temporary bleachers decorated with TRANS FRANCE EXPOSITION banners and streamers were already filled with eager racing fans.

The TV announcer, followed by a TV camera and crew, added to the excitement.

"Ladies and gentlemen — from the looks of this fine crowd, I'd say most of Paris set their alarm clocks early this morning. Welcome, everyone, to the inaugural running of the Trans France Race. Your enthusiastic cheers will be echoed in villages and towns from here to Monte Carlo. And through the magic of Telstar, Jackie Sanford will bring you the entire race. He will be following it all for you, mile after mile. At our TV studio a special electronic map will help you see for yourself every exciting twist and turn of the great Trans France. Ladies and gentlemen — Jackie Sanford!"

"Thank you! Jackie Sanford here, ladies and gentlemen. We'll be bringing you complete up-to-the-minute coverage of this great race. We'll be reporting positions of all the drivers straight on through to Monte Carlo by means of our wonderful electronic map, truly a work of genius, devised by Race Commissioner Sir Reginald Harkness."

The TV camera swung to the back wall of the studio where a huge electronically controlled map of the entire country was placed. Each car was shown in small outline with its number electrically lighted. Nearby, Sanford's assistant, Brewster, wearing earphones, sat before a computer-type keyboard. The third man, Sir Reginald Harkness, stood nearby.

Then the cameras returned to the on-the-spot announcer. "This promises to be one of the most punishing races ever. And these drivers know it." He walked along in front of the drivers still doing last-minute tuning of their cars. He passed by Jim and Wheely — but no Herbie stood beside them.

"Right now I'd like a car to tune," Wheely muttered.

Jim nodded. "I hope that Fontenoy fellow hasn't hidden Herbie so well that he can't find him."

Wheely's fists clenched nervously. "Oh boy! I wish you hadn't said that."

"Well, calm down, Wheely. We might as well suit up. At least *we'll* be ready."

Jim got into his racing jump suit easily. But Wheely's nerves were so tight that he put his on backwards. Wrenches, screwdrivers, and all the equipment he carried in the front pockets now jounced oddly at his back. But he didn't notice.

"I'm a mechanic, Jim. And a mechanic's *nothing* without his car. There's a million and one little details for a race. And I pride myself on being thorough." He looked down at his jump suit. "Where're my tools! My *tools!*" he yelled in panic.

Jim's voice was calm. "Wheely, you have them. You've put your suit on backwards."

Wheely shrugged that off. "That's where I was just going to look — naturally. *But where's Herbie?*"

As though to help answer the question, Inspector Bouchet came hurrying up. "Believe me, I'm as concerned as you are. But I'm sure Detective Fontenoy will be here. He's a man you can depend on. Let me check with headquarters again."

He moved off — but not far off. Over by a gasoline truck, two men in overalls marked TRANS FRANCE turned around — Max and Quincey. Each wore dark sunglasses. The Inspector didn't speak. He gave Max a hard stare. Max's shoulders lifted in a shrug, as though to ask, "Where's the car?"

The Inspector understood. "It'll be here," he muttered. "You be ready." He walked away.

Quincey looked puzzled. "Who was that?"

"Double-X, you dummy."

"Double-X? *Him?*"

A short distance away, Diane stood by, watching her mechanic give the Lancia a final tuning. She looked over toward Jim and Wheely. Herbie was not in sight. Had anything really happened to the little car? She hesitated, then walked over to Jim. "Hello," she said, her voice pleasanter than Jim had ever heard it.

"Hi. Er — about last night, I'm sor — "

"*I'm* sorry," she said quickly.

"Not for missing me with that vase, I hope?"

Unexpectedly, she smiled. "No. I was a little uptight, I guess. Probably nervous about the race."

"I was throwing a few brickbats myself," he replied. "And in the wrong direction, too."

Diane twiddled her helmet strap. "Well, right from the beginning we didn't get off to exactly a flying start."

"Herbie and I take a little getting used to, I guess."

Diane stopped smiling. "When you keep referring to Herbie like that, you take a lot of getting used to. By the way, where *is* your car?"

Wheely eyed Diane with suspicion. What was she smiling about? An uneasy idea popped into his head. "What if she's in cahoots with that Fontenoy fellow? Herbie, get here! This is driving me crazy!"

He was almost ready to wring his skinny little hands when Bruno Von Stickle and Gilbert sauntered up. "Misplace your little car?" Bruno asked, smiling sweetly.

Jim grinned. "Temporarily."

"You should kick over a rock or two," Gilbert suggested. "That bug might show up."

"Oh, not under a rock, Gil!" Bruno laughed. "Under a *gravestone*."

Wheely balled his fists until the knuckles were white. "Von Stickle — "

His words were drowned out by the P.A. system. "Attention, everyone. Would all drivers bring your machines to the grid. Five minutes till race time."

Wheely gave Jim a despairing look.

Bruno and Gilbert started away, but not before Bruno smilingly said, "It's just as well, Douglas. You know the saying — 'They never come back!' "

Diane looked sympathetically at Jim and Wheely. "I — I'd better go."

Jim held out his hand. "Good luck, driver!"

Diane looked hard at him, then grasped his hand. "I think you mean that. Thanks." She hurried off to her car.

Many of the racing cars were being pushed into position along the boulevard. There were to be 32 cars lined up in eight rows, four abreast. They would be stretched along a distance of about a block and a half.

"Drivers," the P.A. boomed, "will you please take your positions as quickly as possible."

Max and Quincey looked at each other uneasily. For a very different reason they worried about Herbie's not arriving.

Over at the pit area, all the remaining cars were being pushed out to take their places — all but Diane's Lancia. It wouldn't start. Jim slapped his hand to his forehead. "Oh, no! Look at that, Wheely. That Lancia's waiting for Herbie."

"So are we. And all we need is 'her' hanging around. If he does get here, he probably won't start either."

"Take it easy. Let's go over and see if we can help."

It was the old glaring Diane who looked up at Jim. "I hope you had nothing to do with this," she said angrily.

"I didn't. But I think I can tell you who did."

"Don't. I already know your answer. Your great Herbie. Just don't say it!"

"Right," Jim replied easily. "And I'll say it. Herbie is missing and the Lancia is missing Herbie."

Diane blew up. "Herbie, Herbie, Herbie. You must think I'm an absolute fool. I don't believe in fairy tales, Herbie, or you."

"Pop the hood, will ya?" Wheely asked Jim.

"Now what are you doing?" Diane yelled.

"You want your car started, don't you?" Jim asked.

One of the mechanics held out a box of tools to Wheely. "Save 'em," Wheely replied briefly.

He looked down at the Lancia's engine. "Listen — I know how you feel, but you'd better get over it right now. Forget Herbie. You know why he's not here? He's found somebody else, that's why. He didn't have the guts to tell you, so I'm telling you myself."

Diane glared and the mechanics stared. "Is this guy crazy?" one asked in a low voice. But Jim was getting the idea. He waited quietly as Wheely took out his wallet. "Yeah, yeah. We're talking about the same guy. Ol' Herbie." Wheely bent to the Lancia's headlights and flipped to a picture of Herbie. "There he is. Ol' fun-loving, fickle Herbie." He snapped the wallet closed. "Gone."

Jim leaned into the engine. "He's right. So far, we've had to tell this to a Fiat, a Thunderbird, and an Austin-Healy. It was fun while it lasted. But the truth is — you weren't the first and you won't be the last. So take off!"

Wheely saw the Lancia's headlight lids close sadly. Furious, Diane stepped from her car. She turned to the mechanic. "Please, please! Won't somebody help me?"

One of the men pushed Jim and Wheely aside. "Here. Let me have a look."

As he reached to grasp a connection, the Lancia's engine roared to life. He pulled his hand back and stared in surprise. Jim and Wheely only nodded. Diane turned gratefully toward the mechanic. "Thank you." She stared icily at Jim and Wheely. "I was beginning to think everyone around here was crazy."

Quickly, she got into her car and headed for the grid area.

"Well, so much for the Lancia," Wheely said. "Anyhow, we did our good deed for the day."

"So much for both of them," Jim shrugged.

"Douglas!" a race official called loudly. "Let's go. Don't you realize you've got pole position?"

"I also realize I don't have a car," Jim called back.

"But it'll be here," Wheely shouted. "You can

count on it." He crossed his fingers.

"It better be — and in two minutes! Or you can try again next year."

In the TV station, Jackie Sanford turned to the Commissioner. "What do we do about Car 53, Sir Reginald?"

"The race will go off on time, Mr. Sanford — with or without it."

All cars but Herbie were now lined up. "Attention. Crews will please leave the grid area." The P.A. man repeated this instruction in French, and all the crews left. "Drivers — are you ready?"

Hands rose.

"Gentlemen . . . and lady . . . start your engines."

A fierce roar of revving engines thundered out. The flagman held a green flag high. With a mighty flourish he gave the starting signal.

"A perfect start," announced Jackie Sanford.

"Ladies and gentlemen — the First Annual Trans France has begun! Claude Gilbert, one of the favorites, is the early leader. Diane Darcy in her Lancia is in fourth position. And Bruno Von Stickle is in the middle of the pack — his usual strategic position. He likes to make his move later."

"Excuse me, sir." Brewster, at the computer

keyboard, turned to Sir Reginald. "I don't seem to have a number for the armored car that's stuck at the starting line."

Sir Reginald replied patiently, "There is no armored car at the starting line, Brewster."

"There is now, Sir Reginald," Jackie Sanford said.

Jim and Wheely, at the edge of the grid, could see the van Brewster had been speaking about. "Boy!" Wheely grumbled. "Everybody's getting in the race but us."

The driver, dressed as a uniformed guard and wearing a military hat, waved at them. Jim's eyes sparked. "Wheely, that's Fontenoy! That's US!"

"That's us?" Wheely stared. "Jim, Herbie's a bug, not an armadillo!"

Fontenoy stopped the van in the pit area. "Monsieurs," he grinned. "Your car."

"Yeah, yeah, Fountainhead," Wheely said excitedly. "But where?"

"*Fontenoy*, please," the detective corrected him.

"But where's Herbie? We're supposed to be in a race."

"Be calm, Monsieur." Fontenoy swung open the back door of the armored car. There was Herbie, looking rather high and mighty. But Wheely, so upset that he was jigging up and down, didn't take in what was happening. "I tell you, I've had it with you French," he raved on. "Men, women, and . . . HERBIE!"

Down the short ramp came Number 53, guided by Jim and Detective Fontenoy. Hurrying toward them came a race official and Inspector Bouchet.

"Are we still in the race?" Jim shouted.

The official shrugged. "From the looks of it, you'll be starting and finishing last."

"Quickly!" exclaimed the Inspector. "There is no time to lose." He pointed to the gasoline truck.

"Yeah, gas. Top of my checklist," Wheely cried.

"Let's move it, Wheely!" Jim jumped to Herbie's side.

The Inspector gave a quick look at the gasoline truck attendants, then moved on to a refreshment stand, Fontenoy at his side. "Good work, Fontenoy," he said graciously.

The detective glowed at this compliment from his adored chief. "You know, sir, something occurred to me last night about the diamond robbery."

"Oh?" the Inspector asked politely, but his attention was on the gasoline truck.

"Something that may be very important," Fontenoy began. He followed the Inspector's gaze in the direction of the gasoline truck. "Monsieur Douglas!" he yelled. "Stop!"

The Inspector, who had begun to sip coffee, nearly choked. "What do you mean, 'stop'?" he asked excitedly. "Do not delay them, Fontenoy."

"No delay, sir." He yelled again at Jim. "The tank is full. I filled it myself this morning."

"Thanks!" Wheely shouted back.

Inspector Bouchet tried not to slide to the ground. He hung on to the edge of the refreshment counter for support.

Max and Quincey looked equally stunned as Wheely recapped the gas tank and beamed. "Okay. One down on the checklist and nineteen to go."

Jim grabbed the list and crumpled it. "One down and NONE to go."

"But Jim! His plugs, points, condenser, brakes, and —"

"Wheely, do you want the best car in the pits? Or do you want to win that race? Hop in!"

Fontenoy was still anxiously trying to get his chief's attention. "Sir, what I was going to say — suppose there was a connection between the men who attacked the car and the men who stole the diamond? Sir, I mean — what if they'd hidden the stolen diamond in that car?"

"*What?*"

"If I may suggest, sir — we should have our men search that car immediately."

The Inspector paled. He crumpled his paper coffee cup, squinching the contents in all directions. "*Search!* In front of — uh . . . There's no time, Fontenoy."

"But, sir, the car is still here."

Herbie certainly was. He wove in and out all over the place, although Jim was doing his best to point him in the right direction. "Herbie! What are you doing? The race is out there!"

"I know what he's doing," Wheely said bitterly. "He can't fool me. He's looking for the Lancia."

Over at the refreshment stand, Detective Fontenoy was still hopeful. "Just say the word, sir, and our men and I will search that car from bumper to bumper."

The Inspector got control of himself. "The word is no, Fontenoy. You don't seem to understand that a thorough search will take an hour. And an hour delay would deprive Douglas of any chance of winning a race he has traveled halfway around the globe to enter."

Admiration gleamed in his assistant's eyes. "What a fine sportsman you are, sir. Now I understand exactly how you are thinking. It's your consideration for others."

Jim, still steering Herbie dizzily around the pits, called out to Number 53, "Come on, Herbie. Forget the Lancia. She's gone."

"You heard him right," Wheely shouted. "Gone! Split!"

Herbie came to a dead stop. But not Wheely. "That's right. Took off in that race like you never existed. She wanted me to tell you it was fun while it lasted. But when push came to shove, she shoved off. That's the way women are. Face it! You've been deserted . . . jilted . . . abandoned!"

"Think he heard you?" Jim asked.

Herbie answered for himself. He reared up on his back wheels. WHIZZ. Whipping across the starting line, he raced after the pack. Headstarts meant nothing to his breaking heart.

Inspector Bouchet marched past Max and Quincey. "Too late now. We'll get it at Monte Carlo after the race," he muttered.

Detective Fontenoy hurried up behind him. "Inspector, sir. I — I think you'll be proud of me."

The Inspector turned slowly. "Now what, Fontenoy?"

"I have done exactly what I know you wanted me to do, Inspector. I have notified Monte Carlo. Their police will search the car as soon as it arrives." He threw his chief a snappy salute and rushed on his way.

Behind him, still as a statue, stood a horrified Inspector Bouchet.

Chapter 8

Late-starter Herbie shot down the Champs Elysees and went screaming through the Place Vendome. Far ahead, Diane Darcy was drawing away from her nearest competitor, Von Stickle.

Jackie Sanford, wearing a headset and microphone, looked at the big electronic map. In the far, far, upper lefthand corner was a late entry, Herbie.

Sanford spoke into the mike. "Claude Gilbert is fighting to hold his lead position. Diane Darcy is running well and pressing him. The wily Bruno Von Stickle is coasting in the style he's famous for. Running a far-distant last is the little American entry, Number 53."

Sir Reginald looked up. "Fifty-three? Where did 53 come from, Brewster?"

"From the armored car, sir."

Sir Reginald's voice was slightly cross. "I don't

want to hear any more about that armored car, Brewster."

On the outskirts of Paris, Herbie ripped along the street, trying to catch the pack. Wheely looked ahead and grinned at what he saw. "There're a few of them. Now I don't feel so lonesome anymore."

By the time Bruno Von Stickle and a few others reached the Trans France road sign at the outskirts of Paris, Herbie was passing stragglers, but still within the city limits.

Jackie Sanford informed the fans. "Von Stickle still in the middle of the pack. Moving up to challenge is Jim Douglas in car Number 53."

Sir Reginald gasped. "Fifty-three! Are you certain, Brewster?"

"Certain," came the brief reply.

Cruising along ahead of several cars, Bruno Von Stickle was not ready to make his move. Almost idly, he glanced into his rear-view mirror. His eyes widened. Number 53! Herbie was pulling up close, trying to pass him. Bruno swung wide to the left, forcing Herbie off the road and sending him smashing through a hedge.

On the electronic map, Herbie's outline made little sputterings and sparks. A worried Sir Reginald looked over at Brewster at the computer keyboard. "Brewster! What are you doing to my map?"

"It's car Number 53, sir. It's gone off the course."

"Nonsense. Your circuit's blown a fuse."

As Herbie headed across the field toward a lake, Brewster reported, "Fifty-three's still off course, sir."

Sir Reginald scowled. "Don't be ridiculous. You're off course, Brewster. You've got him heading for a lake and there's no way across."

Even as the Commissioner spoke, Herbie was taking the plunge. Two fishermen in a rowboat looked up lazily as they heard a splash. They saw only ripples on the water. Then suddenly their eyes opened in terror. Wheely was rising from the water like the Loch Ness Monster. "Nice lake you got here," he called over. "How's the fishing?"

The goggle-eyed fishermen stared, speechless with fright.

"We're lost," Wheely explained. "Trying to find the main road. Which way?"

Beneath the lake surface, Jim's voice bubbled up. "Which way?"

Fishing poles shook in the hands of the terrified men. Wheely smiled in a friendly way. "Well, thanks anyhow. We'll find it." He called down into the water, "Right!"

Wheely's head suddenly began traveling to the right. "Left!" he shouted. He then sped off toward the opposite shore. This was too much for the fishermen. They dropped their poles, each picking up an oar and rowing as fast as he could in the opposite direction.

At the closed iron gates of a beautiful drive, a gardener was looking out at the road where the racing cars sped by. He heard a loud sound behind him. He looked around to see Number 53 splashing out of the lake.

Herbie stopped. His doors opened and out gushed water — also Jim and Wheely. Each lifted his goggles. Out poured more water. Both spouted water into the flowerbed plantings and took deep gulps of air. Hopping back in, they came racing straight for the closed gates. Herbie hardly gave the gardener a chance to swing them open before he roared through, on course once more.

He passed car after car before he spotted Bruno's Lazer GT just ahead. A surge of fury swept through his carburetor. Before Von Stickle could have said, "Fifty-three," he was eating Herbie's dust. On the open road, Herbie skimmed along like a marshmallow on wings.

"We're back on the beam, sir," Brewster reported to Sir Reginald.

"Some of us have never been off it," the Commissioner replied in a chilly voice.

Number 53's team was glowing with joy. "Hope they get that trophy to Monte Carlo in a fast jet," Wheely yelled in excitement. "We may beat 'em to it!"

Jim laughed. "Unfortunately, someone put the Alps in the way."

Wheely's spirits were higher than those famous mountains. "The way Herbie's flyin', nothing could stop him . . . including the Himalayas."

High in the Alps, along the Trans France course, two men stepped from a helicopter. Max and Quincey! They strode over to a waiting car parked near a fork in the road, and Quincey hastily dumped out a number of signs marked with arrows from the envelope he carried. "No 'rights,' " he exclaimed in panic. "And Number 53's coming up next!"

Max calmly seized one of the signs and turned it so the arrow pointed right. Quincey hung it over the left-pointing arrow set up by the Trans France officials. Then, clipboard in hand as though checking the racing cars, he waited for Herbie's approach.

Naturally, Jim steered Herbie to the right — a twisting, climbing, no-road kind of road.

In the TV studios, Sir Reginald scowled. "Brewster, what are you doing?"

"That's their position, sir."

"Impossible! Those drivers are intelligent men. Which is more than I can say for some of the people around here."

Though the road was now no more than a twisting lane, Herbie bravely climbed at high speed. He scooted the inside of a hairpin turn and scuffed to a stop.

"Get out the map, Wheely," Jim ordered. "Something's wrong here. Herbie knows it."

Wheely studied the map. "Some road they picked out," he grumbled. "It isn't even shown here. Maybe we should ask directions."

"Who from? A mountain goat?"

"There must be somebody around," Wheely said, opening the door. He stepped out — into nothing! Only by luck did he avoid toppling end-over-end to the bottom of the ravine, thousands of feet below. But his grip on Herbie's door held. Jim pulled him back. "What's wrong, Wheely?"

Wheely swallowed and pointed downward. "Nothing. Nothing. Not for miles!"

"Let me look at that map."

"It won't be on it," Wheely said faintly. "It's just air. Wait! I'll open the sun roof. Maybe I can call out for help from up there."

He stuck his head up and looked around. "Now don't panic, Jim," he called down. "What you'll be hearing next is my yodel." Cupping his hands around his mouth, he sounded a very good "yo-da-lady-hoooo!" It echoed back.

"Hey! Somebody's out there!" he exclaimed. Then his eager look faded. "It was *me*. Say!" he beamed. "I never heard a real echo before. I was pretty good." He yodeled again and again beamed happily.

"Come on, will ya!" Jim called impatiently.

"Just once more," Wheely called down.

He yo-da-lady-hoooo-ed as loud as he could. Suddenly, there was a thunderous rumbling sound. Wheely ducked down, closed the sun roof, and Jim scrunched close to the wheel. Herbie began to shake as the earth quivered beneath them.

Small rocks bounced off Herbie's top. Wheely was thrilled. "See, Jim! Somebody heard. They're signaling that they're on their way to us."

Indeed, somebody was on the way — Max and Quincey in the black sedan. It pulled up in front of them. Out stepped Quincey, gun drawn. Max followed. Both, squeezing close to the inside of the road, came forward.

"They're after Herbie, again." Jim gasped.

Herbie gasped too — in his own way. As the men stepped up, his windshield water squirters moved like gun turrets.

Before Max and Quincey could mop their eyes clear, Herbie had put himself into reverse gear. He backed down the narrow road, came on one short straightaway and accelerated. Unluckily, he slammed into a sizeable rock that had been tumbled from the slope above by Wheely's yodeling. Jim and Wheely, already shaken by their reverse race, jostled back and forth as Herbie bucked like a bronco to get the rock out of the way.

By the time he had it bumped off into the chasm below, Max and Quincey were back in the sedan and coming on fast. But the big car was no match for Herbie. Still buzzing along on a backward course, Herbie two-wheeled it on the turns and curves. And by the time Number 53 spotted a Trans France road sign, Max and Quincey were far behind.

Herbie felt as though he were being rushed out on the main road by a strong tail wind. But it was only the double sigh of relief from Jim and Wheely that blew him along faster.

"Well — back on the beam," Wheely quavered. "How many cars do you figure are ahead of us?"

"Would you believe all of them?" Jim asked gloomily. "Hey! Do I hear a knock in Herbie's tank?"

Color flowed back into Wheely's face. "Anywhere else — maybe. But not in *my* gas tank. Never!"

"I didn't mean to insult you," Jim said tactfully. "I'm probably wrong, anyhow. Just thought it sound like something clunking around in there."

Wheely sat back stiffly. "Well, we either listen to the driver and stop to take the gas tank apart, or we listen to the mechanic and try to win the race."

Jim grinned. "I'm listening to the mechanic. Let's go, Herbie!"

Herbie rose up on his rear wheels, then plunged wildly onward. Right and left he began to overtake cars, weaving dangerously between them, but keeping his paint job intact, in spite of all peril.

In the TV studio, Jackie Sanford hoped his voice would hold out until the Monte Carlo finish line. "Diane Darcy still hanging onto a comfortable lead. Michael Hastings has now taken over second place, with Claude Gilbert third. Von Stickle is content to remain in the center of the pack, but he's well within striking distance of the leaders. And that Lazer GT is a powerful car." He paused. "For those of you still interested, Car Number 53, driven by Jim Douglas, has popped up on our electronic map. Douglas is back on the course and is also making surprisingly good time."

In the background, Sir Reginald muttered, "He was never *off* course. There was only one person off course, and he is in this room." He threw Brewster a scowling glance.

Bruno Von Stickle cruised effortlessly along the French countryside. He was so confident about winning that he smiled even though no one was around to see his handsome teeth. He glanced into the rear-view mirror and the smile faded. Number 53 was pulling up fast! And before Bruno could believe it, Herbie was side-by-side with the Lazer GT.

For the first time, Bruno looked grim. It looked as though Herbie was going to pass! Then above the roar of engines, he heard a loud sputter. Herbie faltered, slowed down, and Bruno shot ahead.

"Jim!" Wheely yelled. "Make your move! This is no time to slow down!"

"It's not me. It's Herbie," Jim shouted back. "Something's wrong."

Wheely checked the oil gauge. "Pressure's up. Nothing wrong there."

"And we've got plenty of gas."

Herbie greeted this remark with a sad splutter, and his engine began to miss. Wheely's face tensed in worry. "Yeah. Plenty of gas. But he's not getting it."

In his rear-view mirror, Bruno Von Stickle's smile bloomed again. Car Number 53 had staggered off to the side of the road.

As Herbie came to a sad, coughing stop, Jim and Wheely jumped out. Overhead came the chopping sound of a helicopter. Jim looked up. "Sounds like the Trans France wrecking crew."

With all his lung power, Wheely shouted at the sky. "Back off, you vultures! I can take care of it." He flung his arms up to head off the whirlybird.

Several racers they had overtaken sped by. "Wheely — hate to mention it again, but I did hear a knocking."

Wheely spun around. "You mean that nonsense about the gas tank? Well, let's get it straight — once and for all. Who's the mechanic around here, anyhow?"

He walked over to Herbie's gas tank, took off the cap and rolled up his sleeve. He plunged his hand into the tank. "You say it's the gas tank and I say it isn't the gas tank." His hand closed around the diamond. "See? It isn't the gas tank. It's this rock that was *in* the gas tank." He flung back his arm to pitch out Herbie's "stopper."

Jim leaped forward and grabbed Wheely's wrist. "Stop! Wheely, that's no ordinary rock. There's only one kind of rock that glitters like that!"

Wheely almost snorted. "Yeah. Quartz. You can find millions of them in any quarry around Philly." He cranked up his arm for a second try at pitching, and Jim grabbed him again.

"Wheely, you don't find one there worth six million dollars!" He took the stone from Wheely's hand. It sparkled brilliantly in the sunshine. "L'Etoile de Joie!" he exclaimed in an awed voice.

"Are we going to stand around here gazing at a hunk of quartz?" Wheely demanded. He snatched the "quartz" from Jim's hand. "I've seen plenty of quartz, and take it from me —" He stared at the water-clear, sparkling gem. He swallowed. "And take it from me — that's the biggest hunk of diamond I've ever seen in my life!" Like a hotcake he dropped it back into Jim's hand.

"But how did it get there?" Jim asked, stunned by the discovery. Then he sprang to life. "The black sedan! That's why it's been after us. Probably the guys driving it stole this. Probably they dropped it into Herbie's tank to hide it right afterward."

"Afterward what?"

"Don't you remember? There was a robbery at the museum. Everybody was searched. Those guys weren't out to knock us out of the race. They were trying to get the diamond out of Herbie!"

A voice behind them spun them around. "And

thank you for helping us. Up with the hands, please." The voice belonged to narrow-eyed, sneering Max. He faced them, gun drawn.

"You gave us the slip — yes. And for the last time." Quincey grinned in an ugly, joyless way.

Max held out his left hand. "We'll take the rock."

Wheely tried a jolly laugh. "I don't suppose you'd believe that's a big hunk of quartz."

The two stared coldly, silently.

"No," Wheely sighed. "I didn't think you'd be as dumb as I was."

Max waved the gun. "Come on. The rock." He held out his hand to Jim. "Let's have it — now."

There was a moment of dead silence — but only a moment. Herbie had come to France to race and this was not his idea of racing. Besides, he had lost his beloved Lancia. His temper not only rose, it surged straight through his exhaust pipe. Like blasts from a rifle, Herbie shattered the air with deafening backfires.

Max and Quincey whirled around to defend themselves from unseen attackers. And in that instant, Jim made a lunge for Max, knocking the gun from his hand.

Wheely rushed on Quincey, grabbing his arm in a judo hold. Alas! Wheely at his physical peak was no match for his large, would-be victim. Quincey merely straightened the skinny arms that held him. He picked up featherweight Wheely, hurled him to the ground, and bent over him menacingly.

What a target! Herbie rolled up like a butting goat and toppled Quincey. Over the big man went, sailing spread-eagled through the air. *Thump*. He landed at the bottom of the deep roadside embankment.

Wheely sprang up. "Thanks, Herbie. I was gonna do that as soon as I got up."

Jim didn't have such good luck with Max. He threw a solid right, knocking Max to the ground — practically on top of the gun. Max lost no time snatching it up. Victory was in his hands! Jim couldn't help agreeing, staring as he was into the muzzle of the nasty-looking weapon.

But at his moment of triumph, Max's pocket watch sounded its alarm bell. Without thinking, Max looked down as he'd done so many times before, and reached into his pocket to silence it. That was his mistake!

Jim, the diamond still clutched in his fist, was on him like a thunderbolt. Just one old-fashioned "one-two," and Max went tumbling down the embankment to join Quincey. Jim once more had the gun.

Wheely strode up, brushing his hands as

though he were whisking off crumbs. "Well, what do we do with 'em now, Jim?"

Herbie popped his hood and a coil of rope spelled out.

"Right, Herbie," Jim grinned. "We tie 'em up."

Chapter 9

Jackie Sanford's voice was still holding up in spite of the miles it had covered.

"Diane Darcy is still holding on to first place," he announced. "But look out! Here comes the favorite — Bruno Von Stickle. He has moved out of the pack and is bearing down on the leaders."

Sanford glanced up at the map. "He's in fourth . . . moving into third place. Look out ahead!"

Brewster, at the computer, glanced at Jackie. "Excuse me, sir. But Car 53 is now —"

Sir Reginald fought to keep his voice below shouting level. "Brewster, I'm warning you. I've had it with you and that little car!"

Herbie, caring not one snap of his fan belt about Sir Reginald's opinion, whizzed along the Trans France course, carrying Jim and Wheely ever closer to Monte Carlo.

"At least we're back on the road," Wheely sighed.

"And now we've got to get back in the race," his partner said, determination in his voice.

Herbie, his gas tank feeling more comfortable than it had since his first morning in Paris, overtook several cars and went speeding onward.

Back at the scene of their failure, Max managed to crawl his way up the embankment and struggle into the helicopter. He knocked over the phone and talked into it. "Double-X? We lost 'em. First time we ever got done in by a car. Yes, I said car."

Inspector Bouchet looked grim. "Go on."

"The goods'll be in Monte Carlo in a couple of hours. No way to stop them now."

Bouchet did not bother to reply. He slammed down his phone and pressed the intercom button. "Get me the airport." *Slam*. He nearly smashed the phone in his rage. "Why do I have to take care of everything?"

Herbie had never been happier. Ahead of him was the Lazer GT — but not for long! Herbie buzzed by the astonished Von Stickle. Number 53's rear bumper was an unspoken message: "That for you, Von Pickle!"

Now to knock off Gilbert's Pantera II! Herbie shot ahead. Gilbert looked just as stunned as Von Stickle when Number 53 whistled past *him*.

Jackie Sanford's voice came on. "Amazing as it

may seem, ladies and gentlemen, the little car, Number 53, has come out of nowhere to take second place from Claude Gilbert. And at the rate it's going, it looks like a winner. I can't believe it."

Neither could Sir Reginald. "Brewster, you've sabotaged my map for the last time!"

"It's not me, sir. It's the car. I've never seen anything faster."

"Well, you will, Brewster. YOU! Out of here! Fast!" The Commissioner pointed toward the door.

"Soon as we get to Monte Carlo, sir," promised Brewster.

Unaware of Brewster's troubles, Herbie raced along beside a canal. Wheely beamed. "We've passed everything on the road!"

Jim didn't smile. "Except the Lancia."

"Well," Wheely began, looking relaxed, "after the way she jilted Herbie, that's one car he won't want to come in second to. Right, Herbie?"

"Hey!" Jim exclaimed. "Isn't that the Lancia up ahead?"

"Sure is. And it's off the road."

Herbie zipped past. But even so, Jim and Wheely had a quick, horrifying glimpse of Diane's car. It was partly in the canal — and no Diane Darcy in sight!

Jim slowed. "Maybe we ought to stop."

"Stop! And throw away a hundred grand and the biggest comeback of our lives? Jim — we've got it. We're a shoo-in."

"She's in trouble," Jim said stubbornly.

"Plenty of cars get in trouble. Didn't we? Let the rescue boys bail her out."

" 'Bail' is right. There's water in that canal. She could be in real danger. Sorry, Wheely. The comeback comes second!" He tried to turn the wheel. No luck.

"Herbie doesn't seem to think so," Wheely said easily. "He's just buzzin' along."

"Sure. Why should he want to stop after that pack of lies you told him back there?"

"SSHHH!"

Too late. Herbie began to slow down. "Aw, Jim! Now look what you've done!" Wheely nearly cried.

His desperation didn't stop his partner. "Yes, Wheely — Herbie, the jilted lover! If Herbie knew that Lancia had been waiting for him at the starting line . . . if he'd known she wouldn't even budge till you lied about him throwing her over — well, he'd be back at her side right now."

The steering wheel almost pulled from Jim's hands. Herbie made the fastest U-turn ever. Wheely was thrown under the dashboard. He picked himself up as Herbie retraced his own tracks. "I hate to say this, Jim, but you got a big mouth. Sometimes I think it's almost as big as my mouth."

Herbie pulled to a shuddering stop by his trapped beloved. The Lancia's front end was under water and slowly sinking into the ooze of the canal. One glance and Jim could see Diane behind the wheel, frantically trying to open the jammed door. Water was rising higher every second — all the way to her chin!

Jim shouted from the road edge, "We'll get you."

She looked out, tried to speak, and could only sputter, coughing a mouthful of water.

"Try to keep your mouth shut for once," Jim yelled down cheerfully. Then he and Wheely plunged into the canal and struggled with the door.

Water was almost up to Diane's nose by the time they forced the door open and pulled her out. The three struggled up to the road.

"Thanks," Diane gasped.

"You okay?"

"I think so," replied the sopping wet driver of the Lancia. "Missed a shift. Lost control."

"You could've lost a lot more than that," Jim said quickly.

Wheely for the first time looked over at

Number 53. "Hey, Herbie! What're you doing?"

That was a silly question, as it was plain to all three what Herbie was doing. He was backing up to the Lancia — *clank!* — to lock bumpers. Herbie's wheels spun as he tried to pull back to the road.

Diane's face froze in an astonished stare. She looked from Jim to Wheely, then back to Herbie.

"Herbie," Wheely pleaded. "There's no time!"

"Forget it, Wheely," Jim sighed. "He's going to get his girl friend out of the mud — and that's that."

Gilbert's Pantera II roared by.

"And he's gonna get us out of the race," Wheely mourned.

With a mighty effort, Herbie yanked the Lancia to safety. Diane shook her head. "I saw it, but I don't believe it!" she said slowly.

Bruno Von Stickle's car zoomed up and onward.

"Well, you can believe that." Wheely nodded at the Lazer GT's vanishing outline. "We're now out of the money." He looked hard at Jim. "Because sometimes a comeback comes second!"

"Who's giving up? Not me!" Jim replied. "Come on, Diane, you're coming with us."

"Thanks, but I'm staying with my car."

Herbie, now alongside the Lancia, cut his engine. Overhead came the sound of a helicopter marked TRANS FRANCE RESCUE. It hovered over them.

"The rescue guys will take care of us," Diane said as two more racing cars sped past the group. "You two and Herbie try to catch up." She looked up at the copter and blinked back the tears of disappointment. "We'll be in Monte Carlo before you. See you there."

Before Jim could make any reply, she walked over to Herbie. "Herbie, listen to me. I know just how you feel. And I also know you're not a quitter. Now get out there and show 'em you can do it. Win it for them, Herbie."

As a forlorn "toot" came from the Lancia's horn, Diane added, "Win it for *her*, Herbie."

Jim and Wheely stared. Diane understood! And so did Herbie. His engine roared to life. Jim turned to the Lancia's owner. "Diane, I hardly know how to thank —"

Diane cut in. "The rest is up to you," she said, not a wobble in her voice. She looked up at him and before Wheely's and Herbie's amazed gaze, gave Jim a quick kiss. "Good luck!" she whispered.

Another car whizzed by. "Jim! Will ya come on?" Wheely begged. "Everything's all set now, thanks to Diane. Come *on*."

As Jim fitted himself behind Herbie's wheel, Wheely tried to open the other door to get in. It wouldn't budge. "Okay, Herbie. I know you're sore at me about what I told you." He tried again. "Herbie, please. Okay, okay . . . I did it for us. What do I have to do? Get down on my knees?"

Nothing happened.

"Okay." Wheely dropped to his knees. "I lied to you, and I'm sorry. I promise I'll never lie to you again."

The door flipped open. Wheely scrambled to his feet. "Boy, you don't forgive easy, do you?"

In seconds, they were off, waving to Diane.

In Monte Carlo, Inspector Bouchet opened a door marked MONTE CARLO POLICE. The chief, a heavy looking man in his fifties, looked up from his desk. "Bouchet! What are you doing here? Did you miss a turn on the way to the Eiffel Tower?"

"No. A little unfinished business, Emile."

"You have wounded me, old friend. You think I can't handle a little diamond search? Five of my best men are waiting for the cars to enter Monte Carlo. Your assistant, Fontenoy, made everything quite clear to us."

"That is just why I'm here," the Inspector replied.

"Ah ha!" the chief chuckled. "Afraid I will steal some of your glory."

Inspector Bouchet sighed. "There is no glory to be stolen. I wish to make up for a terrible mistake and save everyone from embarrassment. The search is off."

"Off!"

"The message to you was an error by an over-zealous young detective on my staff. Fontenoy was anxious to make an overnight reputation for himself."

The chief frowned. "Ah, yes. I understand. Still — for this kind of news they invented the telephone. Why did you trouble to bring it in person?"

"This is a matter that needed my personal attention. Who knows what complications could arise from a situation like this? Possibly, even an international incident."

The chief shrugged. "Well, it certainly does seem your young assistant has caused you a lot of trouble."

"I assure you," the Inspector said sternly, "I intend to put an end to it."

"Yes, you are right." The chief sighed. "Wiser heads are always called on to clear the mistakes of the young pups. And our reward?" He rolled his eyes toward the ceiling. "We get it when we reach heaven."

Inspector Bouchet's eyes glittered. "Perhaps, in this case, a bit sooner," he mumbled softly.

In the Paris TV studio, Jackie Sanford watched Number 53 streaking along toward Monte Carlo. "It's impossible, ladies and gentlemen."

He stared hard at the map. No mistake about it! "The little car seems to be moving along at a speed no car could possibly attain," he said. Off the mike he spoke to the Commissioner. "Maybe there is something wrong with the map, Sir Reginald?"

Sir Reginald, leaning over Brewster's shoulder to see the computer keyboard, looked a little frantic himself. "Something wrong with my map? How dare you! There's something wrong with that car!"

In a fit of anger, he ran his fingers across the entire keyboard. Instantly, every car on the map went haywire. As the small lights flashed, danced, circled, and streaked, Jackie Sanford tried to smooth over this strange and unexpected turn of events.

"Uh . . . forgive us, ladies and gentlemen. We seem to be having a few little technical difficulties. Please do not try to adjust your picture."

But as he spoke, the situation on the map became so wild that viewers almost forgot about the race. Lights clustered and separated in wild patterns. Some viewers were sure they could make out the likeness of Donald Duck diving through clouds. Others swore they could see Napoleon sliding down the Eiffel Tower. And through all this the most alarming pops, gurgles, and sputters erupted from the map.

"We seem to be losing our audio, too," Jackie Sanford explained wearily. "Don't try to adjust your sound. Stay with us, ladies and gentlemen. I'm sure the situation is only temporary. Stand by."

But almost before he could say "stand by," the entire map exploded. Before the astonished eyes of thousands, only billowing smoke rolled across their TV screens. "Stand by!" the unseen Jackie Sanford gasped. "Just a technical difficulty."

Viewers stood by if for no other reason than to learn what was happening on their screens. Once again, Jackie Sanford's voice came gamely through on their sets. "I know you can't see us, but we're still here, and can still bring you the exciting race over the good old radio waves."

Luckily for the viewers, they could not see the sad sight in the TV studio. It was almost demolished. The three men had escaped any real injury, but their clothes were tattered and scorched. Saddest of all was the proud Sir Reginald. Not only was the pride of his life blown to smithereens, but his mind seemed to have blown along with the map.

Gently, Brewster patted him on the shoulder. "Time to go, Sir Reginald. Don't you worry. Same thing happened once at Indianapolis. Take it easy, sir."

Jackie Sanford watched the two leave the studio, and wished he could leave, too. "Hold everything, ladies and gentlemen," he said, trying not to cough. "We've made contact again. I think I'm getting a report now. Yes! Uh . . . the American astronauts have just swum the English Channel in record time." He shook the earphones. "Don't go away, fans," he begged. We're going to keep trying . . ."

Chapter 10

Unlike the desperate sportscaster, Bruno Von Stickle was in an excellent mood. He had made his move, passed car after car, and only Claude Gilbert stood between him and victory. Luck was with Bruno! As he raced the Lazer GT around the switchback turn, there was the Pantera II — pulled off the road hood up.

He slapped the steering wheel joyfully. "Nothing ahead now but Monte Carlo and victory!"

As Jim, Wheely, and Herbie whizzed to the top of the switchback Bruno had just covered, they were the next to see that Gilbert's chances seemed to be over. "We still have Von Stickle ahead," Jim said tensely. "Come on, Herbie!"

Herbie almost flew on the downhill stretch. Bruno was already taking the second switchback to the lower road — and all Monte Carlo lay ahead! Smiling, relaxed, he glanced up into the rear-view mirror. The smile froze, his muscles tensed! There was Herbie, peek-a-booing around the second switchback and closing distance every second.

Spectators were lining the road now, and if anything inspired Bruno Von Stickle to show his best racing skills, it was spectators. Left to right, right to left, Bruno swung his powerful car to block Herbie's best efforts to pass.

"The dirty road hog!" Wheely shrieked in excitement. "Why doesn't he learn how to drive!"

"He knows how to drive. That's our trouble," Jim bit out.

Wheely looked at the narrowing old streets they were now approaching. A hairpin turn lay dead ahead. "I see what you mean. We're not exactly on easy streets."

Both Number 53 and the Lazer GT took the wild turn, Herbie on two wheels. Now the spectators along the stretch screamed in excitement.

"If we don't get him before the tunnel — " Jim began.

"Don't say it," Wheely begged. "Drive. Herbie! Get him!"

Small chance. No sooner had both cars blasted out of the turn than Bruno again began weaving — and the tunnel hardly inches away!

Bruno shot into the tunnel entrance, and

Wheely's heart nearly broke. "Too narrow!" he almost sobbed. "Herbie can't pass him here."

"Bruno was right." Jim's voice was bitter. " 'They never come back.' That's what he said." He slowed speed and his fingers loosened on the steering wheel.

That was all Herbie was waiting for. He jerked the wheel right out of Jim's hands, pulled the accelerator to the floor, and went RIGHT UP THE WALL!

"Herbie!" Wheely screeched as he was flung against the door. "You'll kill us!" He closed his eyes.

"Not Herbie!" Jim gasped loyally, leaning into Wheely's shoulder. But his eyes, too, were squeezed shut.

They weren't sure if Herbie passed Bruno on the ceiling or made it by gravity-defying roller-drome stunting, but pass him they did.

Two pale, very happy guys zoomed out of the tunnel and streaked across the finish line.

Crowds screamed their approval. They even had a kind look for the stunned, glassy-eyed driver of a second-place Lazer GT.

In the crowd, Inspector Bouchet looked on with much interest as Herbie came to a stop. Jim and Wheely, overjoyed, had no time to spot the Inspector's familiar face.

"We did it!" Jim shouted.

"Never come back, huh?" Wheely shouted back.

Jim grinned. "Guess Herbie wasn't listening!"

They hardly managed to get out of Number 53 before they were being hugged, kissed, cheered, and generally tugged around by admiring fans and race officials.

"A toast to the victors!" somebody cried — but not Inspector Bouchet. He watched, waiting to make his move.

Finally the crowd dwindled down, leaving Jim and Wheely holding a huge golden trophy. Wheely patted the trophy.

"Some cute little memento you got there, old buddy."

"Remember, Wheely — this trophy is as much yours as it is mine. And more Herbie's than ours."

"Yeah! Let's raise a toast to Herbie!"

They moved off in Herbie's direction, but suddenly Jim stopped. "Hey! Wait a minute. There's a little matter of a diamond we've gotta attend to."

Inspector Bouchet knew it was time to move over to Herbie, too. He hurried up just as Jim and Wheely were opening Herbie's doors. "Monsieurs!" he called out. "May I add my congratulations?"

"Inspector!" Jim looked over, surprised. "Say, you'll really want to congratulate us when you see what we have for you!"

"Found it myself," Wheely grinned. "It was right in Herbie's gas tank. I guess if it hadn't been for me — uh . . . well" — he glanced at Jim — "uh . . . I got a hint from another source."

Jim chuckled. He took the diamond from his pocket and held it out. L'Etoile de Joie flashed fire in the light. "This what you've been looking for, Inspector?"

Inspector Bouchet's lips quivered, his eyes glistened, and even his hand trembled as he reached out for the beautiful gem. "Ah, yes!" he murmured, trying to keep his voice steady.

"It's had a rough trip," Jim said. "But luckily it's winding up in the right hands."

"Indeed it is!" the Inspector exclaimed, trying not to snatch the diamond right out of Jim's hand.

Not an inch short of his goal, the Inspector's hand stopped as though by some mysterious force. A voice he had begun to think of as belonging not to Detective Fontenoy but to Detective Disaster sounded almost at his ear.

"Don't know how we missed connections, sir," Fontenoy bubbled in his usual eager way. "But here I am!"

Horrified, Inspector Bouchet turned. There

stood his loyal assistant with the museum's curator, Monsieur Ribeaux.

"F-Fontenoy!" the Inspector gasped. Stinging tears nearly took the place of the gleam in his eyes of only a moment before.

And Monsieur Ribeaux was almost in tears too — tears of pure joy. He grabbed the Inspector's shoulders and, hopping wildly up and down, kissed him on both cheeks.

"You see?" Detective Fontenoy pointed to the diamond. "I knew L'Etoile de Joie would be found. It is an honor to be at your side in this moment of triumph, Inspector." He gazed into his chief's eyes. "And I have even more good news, sir. The two thieves have been captured."

Inspector Bouchet tried to pull his toppling world together. "Good, good. Then I would say the case is concluded."

"Concluded?" Jim looked puzzled. "If you buy the idea that the diamond was stolen by a couple of stooges who got outsmarted by a car, I guess the case is concluded. But it seems to me there must have been a mastermind behind all this."

"Either that, or the museum had some pretty lousy security," Wheely added.

Detective Fontenoy exploded. "Sirs! Men have been challenged to duels for such an accusation. The museum's security was foolproof!"

"Then how did a couple of fools prove it wasn't?" Jim shot back.

"That remains to be told," Fontenoy answered. "And I was just about to tell it." He turned to the Inspector. "I made an interesting discovery just today, sir."

"Uh. . . not now, Fontenoy. We must keep police matters private, you know."

For once his loyal assistant didn't seem to get his chief's order. He went on. "As I was about to say, sir — from the sensitized floor to the radar beams surrounding the pedestal, and even on the pillow upon which the diamond rested, all the traps were thought up and worked out by one man."

"Yes, Fontenoy. But as I said — *later*."

But the eager detective was not to be stopped. "No sir. It is right to give credit where credit is due. The combinations to the entire security system were devised and known only to you, sir. You get the credit. But — "

"FONTENOY!" Inspector Bouchet paled.

"But, as I was about to say, who besides the Inspector knows these details? Monsieur Ribeaux knows only which numbers to push. Who, then, knows all? Who besides the Inspector? No, sir. The case is not closed."

There was a deadly silence. Then Jim and

Wheely burst out as one voice. "Who . . . besides the Inspector?"

Ribeaux's eyes rounded in shock. "It cannot be," he muttered.

But Fontenoy's eyes not only rounded in shock — his mouth formed a large, matching "O." "My chief!" he groaned. "Oh, *no!*"

Inspector Bouchet sized up the situation in one glance. After all, anyone who could think up a foolproof security system was no fool himself. There was only one way out and he knew it. In one swift motion he drew out his revolver. "Who besides the Inspector?" he repeated. "The answer to that question is *nobody!*" He paused and glared at all four men. "My retirement has been delayed too long. Now I hope no one will be foolish enough to make a move."

He turned to make his getaway. Too late! Herbie rolled forward and rested his front tire across the inspector's shoe.

"Move that ridiculous car!" the Inspector bellowed, waving his gun at Jim, "or I will be forced to kill you!"

There was only one answer to such a threat and Herbie made it. With one flip of his hood he knocked the gun from the Inspector's hand. It sailed straight toward Wheely. Shakily he grabbed it. He leveled it toward the Inspector.

Jim quietly stepped up and slammed Herbie's hood down. "Thanks, Herbie," he said briefly. He looked at the Inspector. "Even a mastermind can be outsmarted by this car, Inspector." He held onto the diamond as Detective Fontenoy walked up to his adored chief.

For some reason, Fontenoy's sorrow had suddenly turned to great joy. He smiled proudly. "I always hoped you'd be present when I cracked my first big case, sir. And you are!"

Bouchet's whole body shook as he tried to control his rage. He clenched his fists together and brought them up as though he meant to crush Detective Fontenoy.

The detective reacted quickly and rather strangely to this threat. "Oh. Oh yes. Excuse me, sir — and after all you've taught me, too!"

Fontenoy whipped out handcuffs and snapped them on his chief's wrists. "We'll be off now, sir," he said politely.

Jim, Wheely, and Monsieur Ribeaux stared after the departing pair.

Jim, turning to the museum curator, handed him the diamond. "I believe you'll find it's all here, Monsieur."

Monsieur Ribeaux's eyes gushed wetly in gratitude. "I am so happy," he sobbed. "I, personally, will see to it that this magnificent au-

tomobile receives the greatest honor France can
bestow! Until then — "

He bobbed downward and planted a kiss on
either side of Herbie's hood.

For one incredible moment, it looked as though
Herbie had received a new paint job along with
the kisses. For he blushed crimson. Then, to the
relief of all, he paled back to his usual white.

Ribeaux hastily searched for a handkerchief to
mop his damp face. No luck. Wheely quickly
handed him a grease rag from one of his many
overall pockets. Instantly, the little curator's
tears stopped rolling. "Thank you, thank you," he
replied politely. "But I would not soil your magnificent handkerchief."

He bowed politely and departed, wiping his
face on his cuff.

Chapter 11

Jim and Diane stepped out from a beautiful Monte Carlo restaurant into an even more beautiful moonlit night.

Diane rested her hand lightly on Jim's arm. "Can you believe that all in the same day you saved me from drowning, and possible starvation?"

Jim laughed. "Don't give me too much credit. I don't imagine I'm the only guy in this town who wanted Diane Darcy to have dinner with him."

"Well, it was a wonderful dinner." She hesitated. "I mean, being with you was wonderful."

Jim patted her hand. "Thanks. Matter of fact, I just realized it was wonderful being across a table from you. That's a pretty big change for us."

Diane laughed. "You mean, without Herbie chasing my Lancia?"

"Or your Lancia chasing my Herbie," Jim

grinned. He looked at her. "And another big change, too."

"What?"

"Well — er — you look pretty nice without a helmet, and I like what you're wearing, too. Not that you don't look great in a jump suit, but —"

"I know what you're trying to say," Diane nodded. "But — oh, well, maybe it would be just as much fun if I did spend less time defending myself as a race driver and more time being . . . well, a human being. I mean, a woman human being." She hesitated. "I guess I mean — why can't I be both?"

"I've had a few second thoughts myself," Jim replied. "About me. My ideas, I mean."

They nearly bumped into the doorman at the curb. He looked around, a strange look on his face.

"The little VW, please," Jim said.

The doorman stared. His voice trembled. "Did you say a *VW*?"

Jim looked at him curiously. "Yes. The white one with a "53" painted on the side."

"Yes, yes!" the doorman gulped. "I know it well. It is the toast of all Monte Carlo." But he didn't move to get Herbie.

"Thanks. But it's also our transportation. So if you wouldn't mind —"

"I would not mind, Monsieur, but it is no longer here."

"It was stolen?" Diane cried out in alarm.

"Mademoiselle . . . you will not believe. I would not believe. No one would believe. It was stolen by another car!" He fanned his pale cheeks with his hat. "Impossible!" he gasped.

Jim and Diane looked quickly at each other. He was first to speak. "Now I know that you finally believe what Herbie can do. But you're probably not ready to believe the same thing about your —"

"About my Giselle?" Diane interrupted. "Why not? Giselle can do anything she wants to do."

"*Giselle!*"

Diane laughed. "Giselle and I — we're very strong women. We have our own ideas." She looked up at Jim. "Shall we go find them and make it a foursome?"

"Will we!" Jim hailed a passing taxi. "Take us to the most romantic spot in Monte Carlo, driver."

High above the Mediterranean, a big moon sparkled in the water of the harbor. And high above the water was a small shadowy bench — just the place for Diane to tuck her shoulder close under Jim's arm.

"This is perfect," she murmured.

"Perfect. And we have it all to ourselves

— moon, sea, sky, and Monte Carlo."

A familiar voice came from the shadows. "Being chief mechanic is important. Very important. Of course, I didn't exactly win the race all by myself. But as I said, being chief mechanic is important."

"Oh, *oui, oui*," a girl's voice agreed.

"I did have a little help from time to time," the voice ended modestly.

Diane smothered a laugh. "What were you saying about the moon and everything all to ourselves? I think Wheely's found himself a mademoiselle."

Jim chuckled. "And look over that way," he whispered back.

Diane turned. In the shadows, two sets of headlights blinked gently on and off. Herbie and Giselle!

As they watched, there was a gentle thump of two doors touching.

Softly, the Mediterranean moon beamed silvery light upon two silvery door handles. There was no doubt about it —

Herbie and Giselle were holding doors!